Praise for Irene H

"Irene Hannon wins our hearts with an uplifting story of love and healing."

—***RT Book Reviews*** on *Till There Was You*

"A fine portrait of a heroine faced with true-to-life guilt."

—***RT Book Reviews*** on *A Time to Love*

"A gently paced love story with characters who make you care what happens to them."

—***RT Book Reviews*** on *A Place to Call Home*

"Hannon's multithread plot is woven beautifully together to create a tapestry that will enchant romantics of all ages."

—***Publishers Weekly*** on *One Perfect Spring*

"Inspiring prose and embraceable characters…capture the reader from the very first pages."

—***New York Journal of Books*** on *That Certain Summer*

"Touching, compelling, and satisfying."

—***RT Book Reviews*** on *From This Day Forward*

"A great summer read…relatable characters with real-life problems."

—***Radiant Lit*** on *Seaside Reunion*

"A warmhearted journey from loss and guilt to self-forgiveness and love."

—***RT Book Reviews*** on *Once Upon Nantucket*

"A tender and intriguing tale of heartache, loss, and love."

—***Goodreads*** review on *Crossroads*

"A delightful read...the realism and tenderness draw you into the story."

—***RT Book Reviews*** on *The Way Home*

"An intense, emotional, thought-provoking read."

—***Best Reads (2010-2020)*** on *Child of Grace*

Till There Was You

Circle of Friends—Book 3
Encore Edition

IRENE HANNON

First edition published 1998 by Harlequin Love Inspired as *A Family to Call Her Own*
Encore Edition published 2025 by Irene Hannon
(An Encore Edition is a previously published novel that has been revised and reissued with a new cover.)

ISBN 9781970116502

To Dorothy Hannon,
my wonderful mother and cherished friend,
who gave me Isabel.

1

"That's a lie!" Anger coursing through him, Zach Wright shot to his feet, planted his hands on the desk that separated him from Ted Larsen, and glared at the managing editor. "A total, complete, absolute lie."

"I'm sure it is." Ted's tone remained calm. "But are you willing to reveal your sources to prove you didn't fabricate the information?"

"You know I can't do that." No journalist worth their salt would commit such a breach of professional ethics.

"Then we have to dial back the heat while we work on a game plan."

"Why? My information is solid. I wouldn't use it if it wasn't."

"I know that. But management is getting serious pressure on this. Including the threat of a lawsuit."

Zach gave a dismissive wave. "That's just a scare tactic."

"Maybe. But it worked—for the moment." Ted rested his hands one atop the other on his desk. "It's not easy being a lucrative publisher in this day and age, Zach. You know that. Management is being cautious."

He gave a grunt of disgust. "I can think of a less diplomatic word for it."

"Look, we'll work this out. I know your information is

sound. We just have to prove it." Ted paused. Linked his fingers. "And until we do, we're going to put the series on ice."

Fury bubbling up inside him, Zach jammed his hands into his pockets, strode over to the window, and stared out at the city streets. St. Louis could be beautiful, but on this dreary February day it was ugly—the same as his mood. This whole experience was leaving a very bad taste in his mouth.

He swung back to Ted. "Whatever happened to printing the truth? I thought that was our job."

"It is. But Simmons's job is to keep the paper solvent. As the publisher, he calls the shots. And he's not willing to risk a lawsuit."

"So we just let them get away with it?" He fisted his hands. "The corruption in that office is rampant—misuse of public funds, a rigged bidding process based on nepotism instead of price, blatant bribery—what am I supposed to do, forget about it?"

"No. Just lie low for a while. In fact, why don't you take some time off? How many weeks of PTO have you accumulated, anyway? Five, six?"

"Eight."

"When was your last real vacation?"

"I don't know." Zach shrugged, making no attempt to mask his impatience. "It's been a while." Like three or four years.

"Maybe you're due."

Now? While he was digging into a hot story that got hotter every day?

What kind of journalist did that?

"I don't want to take a vacation in the middle of this coverage." He squared his shoulders. "The story needs to be told, and I'm not running away from it. I'll stand behind my coverage even if the paper won't."

"We're not asking you to run away. Just hit pause. If you don't want to take a vacation while we figure out how to deal with the allegations, we can assign you to another story."

"Like what?"

"The weather folks are predicting that the Ste. Genevieve area is going to get hit with another flood. I need somebody down there to cover it."

Zach's jaw dropped.

Seriously?

They wanted to assign one of the paper's top investigative reporters to a *weather* story?

He gritted his teeth. "You're kidding, right?"

Ted adjusted his glasses, and at the sudden glint of steel in his eyes a red alert began beeping in Zach's mind.

Maybe he'd overstepped.

After all, Ted was his boss. And his usual affable, easygoing manner could be deceptive. Underneath, he was still the tough-as-nails reporter who'd come up through the ranks and who didn't put up with insubordination.

"No, Zach, I'm not." His tone was edged with iron. "You're overreacting to this situation, whether you realize it or not. You need some time to decompress. Nobody can maintain the intensity, keep up the pace you set, month after month, year after year, without wearing down. A change of scene, a different focus, a fresh perspective could be helpful. You can get that by taking the flood coverage assignment—or by taking a vacation. It's your choice. But those are the only options."

* * *

"In one mile, take Exit 154 toward Ste. Genevieve."

As the voice on his phone spoke, Zach frowned and reduced

his speed yet again. With the dense fog, it would be easy to miss the exit ramp and any signs pointing toward it.

He tugged at the knot of silk constricting his throat and drew in a relieved breath as the fabric gave way. Ties were torture devices. But dinner with the publisher was definitely a tie occasion.

To his credit, Simmons had had the guts to discuss the situation with him face-to-face. But even though the publisher had assured him the paper stood behind him and had confidence in his reporting, they'd still hit pause on the series.

As far as Zach was concerned, actions spoke louder than words.

He flexed his taut shoulders and glanced at his watch. Sighed.

Ten o'clock.

It had been a long day. A very long day. And the only upbeat moment had been Ted's parting words.

He played them back in his mind.

"These setbacks happen to all of us, Zach. Don't let it get you down. You're a good reporter. One of the best. We'll work this out."

Satisfying, since Ted's compliments were rare.

In fact...that had been the most satisfying moment in his career for a long time.

Which felt wrong.

Zach frowned and flexed his fingers on the wheel.

His satisfaction used to come from his work. From the feeling he was making a difference.

And that's where it *should* come from. Not from recognition by his boss.

Could that be the source of the discontent, the restlessness, that had plagued him for the past few months?

"Use the right lane and take the next exit."

Zach edged over, squinting as his headlights tried to penetrate the dense fog that was obscuring the lane lines.

In hindsight, given how late the dinner had ended, he should have waited until morning to make this drive.

But that wasn't how he was wired.

He might not be happy about this flood coverage assignment, but doing things halfway wasn't in his DNA. And getting settled in tonight would allow him to dive into the coverage first thing tomorrow.

The sign for Ste. Genevieve loomed out of the mist to his right, and he slowed. Edged onto the ramp when the road veered to the right. Crept along until he hit an intersection. Followed the voice prompt on his phone and turned left.

Man.

This pea soup would do San Francisco proud.

As he inched along the two-lane road toward the French settlement town that was his destination, the shroud of fog insulating him from his surroundings bordered on disorienting. And weird. It was almost like one of those old "Twilight Zone" episodes, and he was the last living creature on earth.

He flicked a gaze to the rearview mirror.

Nothing but fog. No cars, no sign of life.

A shiver rippled through him.

He might not be alone in the world, but he was certainly alone on this ghostly road.

Or maybe not quite as alone as he'd thought.

Because when he redirected his attention to the pavement in front of him, a deer materialized from the mist and bolted into his path.

Uttering a word he rarely used, he jerked the wheel hard to the right, heart stuttering.

The deer bounded off—but as his compact car fishtailed across the unforgiving moisture-slicked asphalt, it seemed to have a mind of its own. Despite his attempt to regain control, it skidded toward the shoulder.

And as it careened off the edge of the road and plunged down an embankment, one stomach-churning thought flashed through his mind.

He'd forgotten to buckle his seat belt.

* * *

Rebecca Matthews stifled a yawn and reached for the cup of coffee in the holder under the dashboard. Grimaced as the cold liquid sluiced down her throat. But she chugged it down anyway. It had been a long day and she needed the caffeine.

She glanced at the clock on the dash. Groaned.

Ten-thirty.

Make that a *very* long day.

Maybe she should have taken her brother up on his offer of a bed for the night when he'd walked her to her car in St. Louis.

Except she'd driven this route a hundred times. And barging in on him just as he and Sam were welcoming a new baby to their family hadn't felt right.

Besides, as she'd assured him, she could make this drive with her eyes closed.

Of course she hadn't meant that literally, but that was close to what she was doing tonight, thanks to the dense, swirling fog.

Tightening her grip on the wheel, she hunched forward and focused on the road. Or what little she could see of it.

So much for her plan to switch to autopilot during the familiar drive. This trek was requiring every ounce of what little energy and concentration she had left. And tomorrow's schedule wouldn't bend to accommodate her late-night arrival home. She'd still have to be up no later than six to prepare for the Friday lunch and dinner crowd at her restaurant. Running out on Rose and Frances today after Brad's call, in the midst of all the Valentine dinner prep, had been bad enough. She couldn't expect them to carry the load tomorrow too.

But she was almost home. Her exit was coming up…if she could see it through the fog.

When the sign at last emerged from the mist, she flipped on her blinker and exhaled. There should be minimal traffic on the secondary highway. Who would be out on such a dismal night, unless a major event like a birth had compelled you to brave the weather?

Maintaining a tight grip on the wheel, she kept close tabs on her surroundings as she drove at a snail's pace, her headlights barely piercing the gloom. Her usual points of reference were invisible, including the homes scattered here and there along the rural road.

She double-checked her gas gauge.

Plenty of fuel to get her home.

Good.

Running out of gas wouldn't be—

She gasped as a figure appeared out of the mist in her headlights, trudging along the edge of the road a handful of feet in front of her car.

She swerved to the left. Jammed on her brakes. Skidded along the slick pavement in the oncoming traffic lane.

When her car finally came to a stop, she looked in her rearview mirror, pulse pounding.

The apparition had been swallowed up in the gloom.

No, not an apparition.

It had been a flesh-and-blood man, wearing a white dress shirt and carrying a suit jacket.

But why had he been walking down the road at this hour of the night in this weather?

Three possibilities flashed through her mind.

He was a lunatic, he was drunk, or he was in trouble.

Her stomach knotted.

She wasn't equipped to deal with any of those situations.

Best plan?

Call 911.

Keeping one eye on her rearview mirror, she guided her car to the shoulder on the right side of the road, confirmed that her doors were locked, and groped in her purse for her phone.

But before she could locate her cell, the man materialized out of the mist again to her left, now walking down the center of the road.

Oh, mercy.

If a car came along, he was a sitting duck.

Yet he seemed oblivious to the danger. And he was weaving, gait unsteady, head bowed.

Heart thumping, Rebecca lowered her window a mere two inches and called to him. "Sir. Sir!"

No response.

She raised her voice. "Hey, mister…you need to get off the road."

His step faltered, and he raised a hand to his forehead. But after a moment he continued on without even looking in her direction.

Now what? He was already disappearing into the mist.

If she took the time to call 911, he could end up in a ditch.

She put the car in gear and drove forward until he came into sight again.

Once she was beside him, she used her loudest voice. "Hey, mister! You need to get off the road."

The man stopped. Peered in her direction.

Though the billowing wisps of fog obscured his face, he was on the young side. Late thirties, maybe. He was also tall. Somewhere in the six-foot range. And he looked fit. Muscular.

A wave of fear left a metallic taste in her mouth.

She'd be no match for someone his size if he had any nefarious ideas, and there would be no one to come to her rescue on this deserted road.

But as the opaque veil between them lifted for a brief moment, it was obvious her fears were unfounded.

The man's pallor was alarming, and there was a long, nasty gash at his hairline. He was in no condition to walk, let alone attack anyone.

She lowered her window even more. "What happened?"

"Accident." He gave a vague wave behind him as he mumbled the response.

Her suspicion meter spiked again.

If there'd been an accident, why hadn't she seen his car?

She rolled her window back up a couple of inches. "What kind of accident?"

"Deer." The word slurred. Then he started walking again.

But after only two wobbly steps his legs buckled and he fell to his knees, palms flat on the pavement.

Enough.

The man needed help, and there was no one here except her to provide it.

Doing her best to rein in her apprehension, she unlocked her door and dashed toward him. Stared at his bowed head while she kept an ear cocked for the sound of an approaching car.

Priority number one was simple. Get him out of the traffic path.

She reached down and touched his broad shoulder. "Look, you can't stay here. You're in the middle of the road."

He gave no indication he'd heard her.

"Please, try to get up." She leaned down and tugged on his formidable bicep. "It's dangerous here."

After a moment, he tilted his head to look up at her with dazed, unfocused brown eyes. "Dizzy." The word was garbled.

"I'll help you, okay?" She tugged harder on his arm.

He frowned. Took a deep breath. Made an effort to stand, leaning heavily on her.

As he struggled to his feet, his intimidating size smacked her in the face. He towered over her five-five frame, and there was strength in his grip despite his injured state.

Another wave of panic washed over her, and for an instant her resolve to play Good Samaritan wavered.

But when she loosened her hold, he swayed.

Not good.

If she didn't help him, he could end up doing a face plant and adding to whatever injuries he'd already sustained.

Gritting her teeth, she guided his arm around her shoulders and tugged him toward her car.

He leaned on her, his breathing labored, while she silently repeated a reassuring mantra.

Stay calm. Be logical. The man is hurt. He doesn't represent any danger.

It was slow going, and by the time they reached her car his complexion had gone from pasty to gray.

She propped him against the front of the hood, brain clicking into gear.

Calling 911 was still an option, but by the time emergency responders got here in this weather she could have him at the ER.

The choice was a no-brainer.

"Stay put." She got in his face and enunciated every word. "I'm going to unlock the car door."

Given his zombielike state, it was hard to tell if her words registered. She'd just have to work fast and hope he was able to remain upright until she returned.

She circled around to the passenger side and lowered the seat to a semireclining position.

The maneuver took less than a minute, but when she backed out of the car the man was trying to navigate around the vehicle on his own.

Uh-oh.

If he fell, he might not have the strength to stand again, even with her help.

She raced toward him, and just when she was within reaching distance he stumbled. Flung out an arm as he tried to regain his balance.

His knuckles connected with her chin.

Hard.

At the backhanded blow, Rebecca gasped. Grabbed his arm to keep from falling herself.

Bad move.

He lost *his* footing and fell against her, pinning her to the hood of the car under his body.

White spots appeared in her vision as panic swept over her.

She was immobilized. At his mercy.

No!

With a strangled sob, she writhed beneath him, struggling to get free. But he was so heavy she could hardly move.

At last, summoning up every ounce of her strength, she shoved him hard enough to create an opening to wriggle free.

The stranger staggered back, eyes glazed. Wavered. Then he dropped to one knee, groaning as he raised his hands to his bent head.

Chest heaving, Rebecca drew in one ragged breath after another as she braced herself against the hood. While tremors coursed through her, the man touched the gash, then stared at the blood dripping from his fingers.

As rational thought returned, Rebecca swallowed past the nausea in her throat.

She'd overreacted. Big-time. This man was in no condition to attack her even if he wanted to, which was unlikely. He hadn't hit her on purpose.

And now he was bleeding again, thanks to her.

Rebecca filled her lungs, then crossed to the stranger, knelt beside him, and scanned his face.

Blood was seeping from the gash, his breathing was labored, and his forehead felt clammy to her tentative touch. The deep grooves etched beside his mouth and the thin, compressed line of his lips suggested he was in pain. Despite the chilly air a thin film of sweat had popped out on his brow.

He was in serious need of medical attention. ASAP.

She lifted his limp arm, tucking her head underneath. Draped it around her shoulders. He probably outweighed her by sixty-plus pounds, so getting him on his feet again wasn't going to be easy. But she had to try. She needed to get him into her car before he passed out, which at the moment appeared to be an imminent possibility.

"You need to stand up." She spoke close to his ear. "I'll help. Lean on me."

She attempted to rise, but he didn't budge. And she couldn't lift a dead weight.

"Come on, mister. Try. Please!"

This time when she urged him up he took the cue.

He swayed once he was upright, but she planted her feet in a solid stance. "We're close to the car door." She urged him forward, trying for a calm tone. "It's only a few steps. You can make it."

Somehow she got him into the passenger seat. Then she retrieved his suit jacket from the middle of the road, tossed it into the back seat, and slid behind the wheel.

As she put the car in gear, she glanced over at him. It was hard to tell if he was conscious, but he was breathing.

And as long as he *kept* breathing, in less than ten minutes she could turn him over to the medical experts in the ER and close the book on this bizarre end to an unforgettable Valentine's Day.

* * *

"And you didn't see anything else?" The police officer looked over at her, pen poised, after Rebecca finished her statement in the ER.

"No. Like I told you, he mumbled something about a deer and an accident. But I didn't see a car."

"We'll check it out." He turned to a new page in his notebook. "Let me get your address and phone number."

She frowned. "Why?"

The officer arched an eyebrow. "If we have any questions later about the statement, we may have to call you."

"I'd rather keep my name out of this."

"We can mark your contact information as confidential, if you prefer. But we do need it for the record."

"Will he have access to it?" She motioned toward the door to the treatment rooms, where they'd wheeled the stranger.

"No."

In that case, there should be no problem.

She gave him the information he wanted as a doctor joined them in the waiting area.

"How is he?" The officer put the notebook back in his pocket. "I need to talk to him."

"He's still groggy. I'm not sure you'll get much, but you can try if you want to. We're going to keep him overnight for observation."

"But he'll be okay?" Rebecca picked up her purse.

"The prognosis is good."

"Is there someone you can notify on his behalf?"

The doctor nodded. "He gave us the name of a friend in town."

Excellent.

She was bone-weary, and six o'clock was going to roll around way too fast. The sooner she could get home the better.

"May I leave now?" She directed her question to the officer.

"Yes."

"He did ask who brought him here." The doctor folded his arms. "I assume he'd like to thank you. Do you want me to pass along your name?"

Rebecca was shaking her head even before he finished. "No."

"Understood. And you're wise to be cautious. You can't be too careful these days."

"That's true." The officer gave her a thumbs-up as she dug out her keys.

With a parting wave, she swiveled and made a beeline for the exit, paying attention to her surroundings as she crossed the dark lot to her car. Caution was always prudent, as the office and doctor had both concurred. But she picked up no danger signals in the lot.

The man in the ER?

Different story.

There was an unsettling aura of risk about him. Not in terms of physical danger, though. It was more like he represented a threat to…to her peace of mind.

Which was absurd.

She didn't even know his name, for pity's sake.

Rolling her eyes, she pressed the auto-lock button on her key fob.

Maybe her weird train of thought had something to do with Valentine's Day. After all, despite his ashen color and disheveled appearance, the stranger had been handsome in a rugged sort of way with his dark brown hair, strong profile, firm jaw, and coffee-colored eyes. He looked like the kind of guy who knew how to romance a woman.

If a woman was in the market for that sort of thing.

She wasn't.

And that made her odd flight of fancy even less logical.

She climbed behind the wheel, started the car, and pointed it toward home. Within seconds, the lights of the hospital where the stranger lay vanished in the mist.

But she had an odd and unnerving feeling that *he* wasn't going to disappear as easily.

2

"Hi, Ben."

As Rebecca slid onto a stool and greeted the rotund man behind the counter, he turned.

"Hi, there." He wiped his hands on his white apron and smiled. "I was beginnin' to think you were going to skip your coffee again this morning. Missed you yesterday."

Rebecca crossed her arms on the counter and offered him a rueful twist of her lips. "I barely made it to the restaurant in time to get lunch going. I don't function well on five hours of sleep. And I don't feel much more rested today."

Ben's bushy white eyebrows headed north. "Late night Thursday?"

"Yes. My brother and his wife had their baby, and I drove up to St. Louis to be with them."

"Everything go okay?"

"Yes. Except for driving home in the dark and the fog."

"I heard it was bad." He squinted at her. Leaned closer to examine her chin. "You've got a nasty bruise. What happened?"

Apparently her heavy application of foundation hadn't been adequate to disguise the bluish patch of skin on her jaw.

"That, my friend, is a long story."

Before he could ask any more questions, the jingling bell over the door announced the arrival of another customer.

Ben lifted a hand in greeting, then poured her a cup of coffee. "This'll wake you up. I'll be back in a minute."

Rebecca took a long, slow sip of the potent brew.

She could easily make her own java at her restaurant a few doors away, but her trips for coffee—peace missions three years ago, when Ben had been one of the few people to oppose her request for a permit to open a restaurant—had become an enjoyable way to start the day and catch up on town news. And once she'd convinced him that her French bistro wouldn't compete with his diner, they'd become the best of friends.

When he ambled back to the counter, her cup was almost empty, and he reached for the pot to give her a refill. "I know one is your usual limit, but you'll have a busy day today, it bein' Saturday and all. You'll need an extra jolt of caffeine." He reached into the toaster oven behind him, withdrew a bagel, and plopped it on a plate with a packet of cream cheese. "Have this too. You need to keep up your energy. Running a restaurant is hard work. I know." He gave her a wink.

Warmth filled her heart. "Thanks, Ben. What would I do without you?"

He waved that aside. "You'd get along fine. You've got those two busybody sisters dithering over you all day at the restaurant."

Her lips twitched, and she hid her amusement behind a sip of coffee. "You know I could never manage without Rose and Frances. They're a godsend."

That earned her a snort as he reached for a damp rag and began polishing the sparkling counter.

The friendly rivalry for her affections between the two camps—Ben in the diner, Rose and Frances in the restaurant—was always entertaining.

She lifted her mug. "I'll say this, though. You make the best coffee in town."

"That's a fact." He pulled the St. Louis paper from beneath the counter. "May as well take a gander while you enjoy my brew. Probably be the only time you sit all day."

As he moved off to serve another patron, Rebecca scanned the headlines, homing in on a story about area flooding. That was always worrisome.

She didn't even look up when the jangling bell announced a new arrival—until Ben leaned down to give her an update.

"Mark's here. Got a stranger with him too."

She glanced into the mirror over the grill.

Stopped breathing.

The stranger with Mark was the man from the fog. And if she'd had any doubts, the bandage on his forehead, peeking below his hair, dispelled them.

She raised the paper to hide her face and peeked above it to give him a surreptitious once-over in the mirror.

His color was back to normal, his dark brown hair was combed, and his worn jeans sat well on his lean hips. Dark hair dotted his muscular forearms above the rolled-up sleeves of his forest-green shirt.

The man radiated an almost tangible—and scary—virility.

It was time to make her exit.

Before she could escape, however, Mark spotted her and walked over, the stranger in his wake. "Hi, Rebecca. May we join you?"

Trying to tamp down the staccato beat of her heart, she angled slightly toward them as they approached, conjuring up a smile for Mark while avoiding the stranger's eyes. "Of course."

Mark climbed onto a stool and hooked a thumb toward his companion. "Rebecca, meet a buddy of mine from my growing-up years in KC, Zach Wright. He's a reporter—for that paper, in fact." Mark tapped the section Rebecca was clutching. "He's here to cover the flood. Zach, Rebecca Matthews."

She was going to have to look at him.

Steeling herself, she took a deep breath and faced him.

During their last encounter, his eyes had been glazed, unfocused, and dull with pain. Now they were clear and alert and warm—and metabolism-disturbing.

Zach held out his hand. "It's nice to meet you, Rebecca." His voice was deep and mellow, with just a touch of huskiness.

She cleared her throat as she placed her fingers in his. "Likewise."

Instead of releasing them at once, he studied her, faint creases denting his brow. "I don't mean to stare, but have we met before?"

She debated how to answer as she tugged her fingers free.

Her rationale for keeping her role in the stranger's rescue a secret because he *was* a stranger no longer made sense.

"Sort of. Although given the circumstances I'm not surprised you're having difficulty placing me. Between the fog and the accident, I'm amazed you remember anything."

Zach stared at her. "You mean…it was you on the road Thursday night? You were the one who stopped to help and drove me to the hospital?"

"Yes."

Mark looked from her to Zach. "Are you telling me that Rebecca is the angel of mercy you've been raving about?"

Angel of mercy?

She shook her head. "That would be a stretch. I just took him to the ER."

"A lot of people wouldn't have gotten personally involved. You get the Good Samaritan award for sure." Mark leaned closer to her. "Did that happen during the rescue? It looks like somebody slugged you."

Rebecca flicked a quick glance at Zach as she searched for a response that wouldn't implicate him.

But he'd already figured it out.

"I did that, didn't I?" His voice was quiet, and the furrows on his forehead deepened.

"It's no big deal." She waved aside his concern. "You were hurt. You lost your balance, and I was in the way."

He expelled a breath and raked his fingers through his hair. "I think I owe you a very big thank-you—and a sincere apology."

"Not necessary. I'm glad I could help. How are you doing?"

"I'm fine."

Mark gave him a get-real look. "Sure you are. If twelve staples and a concussion are fine. Go ahead and grab that seat." He motioned to the stool next to her.

Zach hesitated, sending her a questioning look.

Her pulse skittered.

Sitting next to this man was *not* a good idea.

Somehow she coaxed up the corners of her mouth. "Please take it. Or mine. I have to get to work, anyway." She drained her cup in one long gulp and slid to the floor. "I hope you're back to normal soon."

"Thanks. And thank you again for Thursday night." The husky timbre of his voice short-circuited her respiration. "I'm not sure what would have happened if you hadn't come along. I'm just sorry about that bruise." His troubled gaze flicked to her jaw. "For the record, I'm not in the habit of hitting women."

"I'm sure you aren't. Mark, I'll see you later."

"You bet."

"Ben, thanks for the coffee."

"Anytime."

And then she fled.

Before Zach's compelling brown eyes, which radiated character and integrity, sucked her in any further.

And made her forget that not everyone who looked upright and honorable was principled and noble.

* * *

Zach frowned and planted his fists on his hips as Rebecca disappeared out the front door of the diner.

It was almost as if she'd wanted to escape from him as fast as possible.

Why?

It wasn't that she'd been unfriendly. More like…skittish. And intriguing, with an unusual blend of poise and vulnerability. Rebecca Matthews radiated an almost innate goodness, and an old-fashioned air of shy sweetness.

Not qualities he'd run into often among the women in his circle.

Still puzzling over the odd juxtapositions, he turned to find Mark watching him with an amused expression. "Forget it, pal."

"Forget what?" Zach kept his tone conversational as he slid onto the stool next to Mark and reached for the mug of coffee Ben placed on the counter.

Mark grinned. "I've seen that look before. Had it once myself. Just don't get your hopes up. Rebecca's great—but she has no interest in romance."

"Are you speaking from personal experience?" He took a sip of his brew.

One side of Mark's mouth quirked up. "Of course. Do you

think a single woman who looks like her could come to a small town like this and not be pursued by every eligible man in the county? But she wasn't interested. Period. In anyone. So I didn't take it personally. We all had to settle for being just friends."

"Interesting. But I'm not in the market, anyway. My boss sent me here to decompress."

Mark waggled his eyebrows. "I can think of worse ways. Romance is good for the soul."

"I'll take your word for that. And speaking of romance, when do I get to meet your elusive fiancée?"

"Dinner tomorrow night, if that works for you."

"My social calendar is wide open."

"Great. Listen, do you mind if I duck into the post office while you finish your coffee? Then I'll give you the ten-cent tour of the town."

"No problem."

Mark slid off the stool. "Ben will keep you company while I'm gone. Right, Ben?" He called down the counter.

"Sure."

When the door jangled as Mark left, Ben ambled over to remove his cup. "Nice girl, Rebecca."

"Seems to be."

"Make somebody a good wife." He scrubbed at a spot on the counter, giving him a side-eye.

Curious.

"From what Mark says, the lady's not interested in romance." Zach sipped his coffee.

Ben waved that off. "She just hasn't met the right man yet."

Since the proprietor seemed to be in a talkative mood, and Mark wouldn't be back for a few minutes, why not see what else he could learn about his angel of mercy? The knack he had for discreetly ferreting out large amounts of information without people realizing just how much they were divulging could come in as handy here as it did in his job.

"She mentioned she had to get to work. What does she do?"

"Runs a restaurant down the street that serves fancy French food."

"Is she the chef?"

"Yep. Also the owner."

"Has she been doing that long?"

"'Bout three years now, I guess. People come from all over to eat there. She's had a lot of good press too. Even in St. Louis." Ben rattled off a litany of the publications that had featured her restaurant.

His own included.

"I wonder where she learned to cook." Open-ended comments almost always yielded helpful information.

"Culinary Institute of America. And she worked in a couple of fancy restaurants in other places before striking out on her own."

"She from around here?"

"Not too far away. Little town in southern Missouri, where her father still lives."

"So no family in Ste. Genevieve?"

"No, but her brother, Brad—he's a minister—and his wife, Sam, live in St. Louis. They had a new baby Thursday, and Rebecca went up there for the day. That's why she was out driving so late."

Ben was a fount of information.

"The timing of the baby's arrival was lucky for me." He lifted his cup to signal for a refill, and Ben topped it off. "Too bad she doesn't have any family in town."

"Well, we're all pretty tight around here. We watch out for each other. That's one of the benefits of small-town living. And she's got me. And Rose and Frances at the restaurant. Neither of them ever married, and they dote over her like a daughter."

The bell above the door rang, and Ben glanced over. "Sorry to leave you in the lurch, but I've got to take care of the new arrivals."

"No worries. I'll chill till Mark gets back."

And mull over all the information Ben had been happy to share, which left him more intrigued than ever about the beautiful woman with hazel eyes, russet-colored hair, and classic high cheekbones that were accentuated by her French-twist hairstyle.

When Mark returned, his friend gave him an apologetic look. "Sorry. That took longer than I expected. I hope you weren't bored."

"Not in the least."

In fact, it had been a very productive few minutes.

As they set off on the promised tour, one of the first places Mark pointed out was Rebecca's restaurant—a modest storefront in the historic district, identified only by a discreet awning that displayed the name.

"She's an amazing chef. You should try her place while you're here—if you can get a reservation."

"It's that popular?"

"Yeah. She's usually booked solid for dinner weeks in advance, unless you can snag a cancellation. You may have better luck at lunch."

"I'll keep that in mind."

Because he intended to become a regular customer.

And hopefully become acquainted with more than the gourmet fare.

* * *

"Rose, have you seen the tube of whipped cream with the star tip?"

As Rebecca called out the question, her head stuck in the restaurant's huge refrigerator, Rose glanced at the work counter.

The tube lay in clear sight, right next to the torte Rebecca was decorating. Exactly where she'd laid it moments before.

How strange.

Rose looked at Frances across the counter. Her sister seemed mystified too. Rebecca was extremely organized and never got flustered.

"It's right here, dear." Rose pointed to the tube as Rebecca turned.

"Oh." Her cheeks pinkened. "I, uh, guess my brain isn't in gear this morning. I haven't quite caught up on my sleep since Thursday night."

"Frances and I will finish up in the dining room and leave you in peace to work your magic on that cake." Rose motioned for her sister to follow her.

"All right." Rebecca wiped her hands on her apron and surveyed the kitchen. "Now where did I put that spatula?"

When they reached the dining room, Frances leaned close and spoke in a low voice. "What do you make of that?"

Rose shook her head. "I don't know."

"She almost put cinnamon in the quiche this morning too."

Rose cocked her head. "Do you think it's possible that she…could she have met a man?"

Her sister's eyebrows shot up. "You think she's distracted because of a man?"

"Well, not that I have much personal experience in that

department, but I do read romance novels. And distraction is a symptom of romance. Have you ever seen her so disorganized or absentminded?"

"No. She's always buttoned-up. Could she have a health issue, I wonder?"

"I don't think so. She seems fit as a fiddle." Rose squinted toward the kitchen. "I'd bet my prize-winning recipe for pickle relish that there's a man behind this."

"But who?" Frances looked bewildered. "There's no one new in town."

"I don't know. But that old buzzard, Ben, might. She had coffee there this morning. She may have mentioned something to him."

Frances shook her head. "He won't tell us anything."

"He will if you take him a piece of that torte this afternoon. He has a sweet spot for you, anyway."

"He does not." Her sister's cheeks flushed.

Yes, he did. It was as plain as the nose on anyone's face. But she let it pass. "You could try, anyway."

Frances smoothed back her hair. "Well, I suppose it couldn't hurt to drop in on him."

"That's the spirit. Let's hope he has some useful information."

The lunch rush came and went before Frances could slip away, but once she did Rose kept an eye out for her through the front window.

As soon as she came into sight, Rose bustled over to the door and was waiting when she stepped through. "Well?"

Frances took her arm, drew her into a corner of the restaurant, and leaned close. "There's a new man in town. A reporter. No wedding ring. Rebecca's age. He stopped in at the diner with

Mark this morning while Rebecca was there. Ben said he seemed interested in her."

"Ooh." She clasped her hands in front of her. "Like love at first sight?"

"Not quite first sight."

While Frances filled her in on the events that had transpired Thursday night, Rose kept tabs on the few patrons who were lingering over a late lunch.

"His name is Zach, by the way. And Ben said he seems like a nice gentleman."

"Good job, Frances." Rose gave her a high five. "You could have been a detective. I think our Rebecca may be—"

The front door opened, and a young man carrying a large vase covered with green florist tissue entered the shop and made his way toward them. "I have a delivery for Rebecca Matthews."

"I'll get her." Rose nudged Frances, then bustled toward the kitchen and stuck her head inside. "Rebecca, there's a delivery for you."

She looked up from the soup she was stirring on the stove and frowned. "All our delivery people know to come around back."

"It's not that kind of delivery."

"What does that—"

Rose pushed through the swinging door before she could finish the question and spoke to the courier. "She'll be right out."

Thirty seconds later, Rebecca strode into the dining room. Jolted to a stop when she spotted the young man holding what was obviously a vase of flowers.

"Rebecca Matthews?" The courier started toward her.

"Yes."

"These are for you." He handed her the flowers and headed back to the front door.

As Rebecca gaped at the vase, Rose spoke up. "Aren't you going to open them? Don't you want to know who they're from?" As if she couldn't guess.

"Um…yes. I guess so."

She set the vase on a vacant table and tore off the green paper to reveal a dozen long-stemmed yellow roses artfully arranged with fern and baby's breath.

"Oh, my." Frances touched a petal. "Aren't they beautiful?"

"Here's the card, dear." Rose extracted the small envelope and held it out.

Rebecca took it gingerly. Opened the envelope and slid the card out. As she scanned the message, her cheeks got ruddy again.

"Well?" Frances leaned forward.

Rebecca looked up. Gave them a blank look, as if she'd forgotten she had an audience. "They're from, uh, someone I did a favor for. A thank-you." Then she picked up the vase and scurried back to the kitchen.

As the door swung shut behind her, Frances turned. "Do you think they're from him?"

"Absolutely. Who else would be sending Rebecca flowers?"

"They could be just a thank-you, I suppose. Like she said."

Rose snorted. "Get real, Frances. A bouquet of daisies would suffice for a thank-you. No man spends big bucks on roses unless he's interested in more than friendship."

"So our Rebecca has a suitor."

"That's the way I read it. Now let's hope she gives him a chance."

* * *

"Rebecca, your friends from St. Louis asked if you could stop by their table when you have a minute." Frances bustled into the kitchen to pick up more salads for the first course of the prix fixe dinner.

She turned from the stove where she was stirring the sauce for chicken Madeira. "Tell them I'll swing by at dessert."

"Will do."

Rebecca's lips flexed as she added lemon juice to the sauce.

It would be nice to visit with her childhood friend for a few minutes. It had been a while since Laura and Nick drove down for a meal.

Understandable, though. Laura's business as a landscape architect was booming, and her free time was devoted to the man of her dreams, as she called Nick. And good for her. After the serious problems in her first marriage, she deserved a happy ending.

And thanks to Laura, her brother had gotten a happy ending too. If Sam hadn't been Laura's maid of honor, she and Brad might never have found each other.

Happy endings all around, it seemed.

Except for her.

Stifling that depressing thought, she refocused on the sauce. Her patrons paid a pretty penny for their dining experience here, and their food deserved her full attention.

An hour later, as she shaved dark chocolate on top of the chocolate mousse, weariness began to set in. Thank goodness she'd decided to limit dinner service to a single seating on Friday and Saturday nights. Until she could afford to hire another chef, this was all she could manage. As it was, she felt like a zombie by Saturday night.

But it was gratifying to see all her hard work pay off.

Rebecca stepped back and surveyed the forty servings of dessert.

Perfection.

As Rose and Frances entered the kitchen with two of the high school students who helped out on weekends, she shrugged off her apron, picked up two servings of dessert, and stepped into the dining room.

Nick and Laura were at their usual table, of course—the same one they'd sat at on their first visit, in the early stage of their relationship, and the one they always asked for when they made reservations.

As she joined them, Nick rose and pulled out a chair for her.

"Thanks, but I'm not staying long. I don't want to intrude on your dinner." She set their mousse in front of them.

"You're not intruding. We'd love to visit with you for a few minutes, if you can spare the time." Laura tapped the empty chair. "Please?"

"Well…I'm wrapping up in the kitchen, so I'll stay for five minutes. But no more. You only come this far south at dinner time for special occasions, and three's a crowd."

Laura sent Nick a sidelong look. "Actually, you're the fourth."

It took her a moment to process that—and come to the obvious conclusion. "Does that mean what I think it does?"

"If you're thinking a baby is on the way, yes." Laura looked at Nick, who took her hand in a gentle clasp, his eyes so warm and tender that pressure built behind Rebecca's eyes.

What must it be like to have a man look at you as if you were the only thing in the world that mattered?

Blinking to clear her vision, she reached over and took Laura's free hand. "I'm so happy for you both. When's the big day?"

"September 4, according to the doctor. It seems like such a long way off, but I know the time will fly. And I can't wait to decorate the nursery."

As Laura chattered on, Rebecca fought back another wave of melancholy.

She was thrilled for her, of course. Just as she'd been over the moon for Sam and her brother when they'd welcomed their daughter into the world.

But being in the presence of such committed, loving couples only served to remind her of her own solitary life.

After a few minutes that involved more listening than talking, she forced up the corners of her mouth and stood. "And now I'll leave you two alone to celebrate. Congratulations again."

Nick rose. "Thank you for a superb meal."

"I'm glad you enjoyed it."

"Keep in touch, okay?" Laura took her hand.

"I will. And I'm sure I'll get regular updates from Brad and Sam too. Drive safe going home."

She turned and hurried toward the kitchen, fighting back tears as she berated herself for indulging in a pity party. She had so much to be thankful for. It was wrong to feel sorry for herself. Just because she'd never found someone who had the patience to unlock her heart didn't mean—

"Hello, Rebecca."

She halted as the husky voice that had invaded her dreams for the past week spoke from her right—and played havoc with her respiration.

What was Zach Wright doing here? He hadn't been on the reservation list.

Slowly she angled toward the voice.

It was him, all right. Sitting alone at a secluded corner table.

Unfortunately, it was too late to hide in the kitchen as she had last week when she'd spotted him in the dining room at lunch.

Swallowing, she brushed her hand across her eyes as discreetly as she could and called up a smile before walking over to his table. "This is a surprise. I didn't see your name on the reservation list."

"I managed to snag a last-minute cancellation." Faint parallel lines appeared on his forehead as he studied her with probing eyes that didn't look as if they missed much. Then he rose and motioned to the extra chair. "Could you join me for coffee?"

Rebecca ran her damp palms down the front of her black slacks. "Thank you, but I have a lot still to do in the kitchen and—"

"Nonsense, my dear." Rose paused to refill Zach's coffee cup as she bustled by. "Everything is under control. Go ahead and enjoy some coffee with this nice young man. You've been on your feet all day."

Drat.

"I won't take up much of your time." Zach gave her an engaging smile.

Since Rose had deep-sixed her best excuse to decline his invitation, she was stuck. "All right. For a few minutes." She lowered herself to the chair. Perched on the edge.

"Now isn't this cozy?" Rose beamed at them, then pantomimed a coffee cup to Frances across the room.

Rebecca gave the sisters a dark look, which they ignored.

"If you need anything else, let us know." Rose spoke to Zach as Frances set another cup of coffee on the table, than took her arm and propelled her away.

Rebecca gritted her teeth.

She was going to have to have a long talk with them later if they'd suddenly gone into the matchmaking business.

Zach's mouth quirked up as he watched them hustle about. "They seem energetic—and efficient."

"They are. I couldn't run this place without them. But they take a bit too much interest in my personal life."

"I appreciate them being my allies tonight, but I didn't mean to railroad you into having coffee with me. I feel a bit guilty."

He didn't look it, though.

"It's not a problem. I can spare a few minutes." She smoothed out a wrinkle in the linen tablecloth. "Besides, this gives me a chance to thank you for the flowers. They're beautiful. But that wasn't necessary."

"Yes, it was. You took a risk, stopping to help a stranger, and I appreciate that. And I still feel bad about the bruised jaw. Sending flowers was the least I could do to—"

"So those beautiful roses were from you." Frances halted as she passed. "Rebecca loved them. She even kept one to dry."

Oh, for pity's sake.

Rebecca sent the woman a withering look, heat creeping over her cheeks. "Frances, let's not embarrass a customer." Or a boss.

"Oh, my. I guess I shouldn't have said anything, should I?" Frances clapped a hand over her mouth. "You're supposed to keep a gentleman guessing, aren't you? Well, I'd best leave you two alone before I put my foot in my mouth again."

As she hurried off, Zach grinned. "I see what you mean about personal interest."

"Sorry about that." Rebecca resisted the urge to fan her face. "They're reading way too much into flowers and tonight's impromptu conversation."

Zach took a sip of his coffee, set the cup down, and locked

onto her gaze. "Are they?"

Her lungs lost their rhythm.

His meaning was clear…and dancing around it was silly. Because despite the buzz of attraction between them—on her end, anyway—Zach was way out of her league. Too fast-moving and smooth, reeking of worldly experience, with a deep-seated weariness in his eyes that suggested he'd seen and done it all. "Look, I need to be upfront. In case you have any interest in seeing me socially, I don't date."

He cradled his cup in hands that looked as if they'd be equally at home chopping wood—or caressing a woman. "Why not?"

That wasn't a subject she intended to discuss tonight.

"I just don't."

And that's all she was going to say.

He sipped his coffee. "I think it's only fair to tell you I'm not the kind of guy who gives up easily. Do you mind if I keep trying to convince you to make an exception in my case?"

"You'll be wasting your time." She forced up the corners of her lips to soften her bluntness. "Even if I was interested, you fall into the traveling-salesman category. Here today, gone tomorrow. I'd be nothing more than a pleasant diversion while you're stuck in our small town. That's a recipe for heartbreak."

He took a breath. Let it out. "I understand your concern. And I appreciate your honesty. But Ste. Genevieve isn't that far from St. Louis. And I'm not Harold Hill."

Interesting that he'd caught her subtle reference to one of her favorite musicals.

"Maybe not in miles, but it's a different world. *Your* world. This is mine."

After a moment, his lips bowed. But unless she was

mistaken, there was disappointment in the depths of his irises. “Can we at least be friends while I’m here?”

Every instinct in her body told her that could be a mistake. Because friendship had a way of morphing to more. Yet how could she say no without dinging his ego more than she already had?

“I suppose so.”

His smile warmed her all the way to the tips of her toes. “That’s a start.”

To what?

Before she could ponder that, a patron at a nearby table looked around, credit card in hand, and she excused herself to attend to business.

By the time she returned with the customer’s receipt, Zach’s table was empty, the cash he’d left in his place more than enough to cover his bill and a generous tip.

But even though he was gone, the vitality and energy and virility he radiated continued to vibrate in the air.

She took a steadying breath.

They may have agreed to be friends, but his last comment suggested he had more than that on his mind.

And truth be told, she did too.

God help her.

3

Zach turned up the collar of his jacket and took another sip of steaming coffee from the disposable cup.

While the Red Cross tent offered an oasis of light, it afforded only marginal protection from the cold drizzle and bone-chilling wind that sliced through the darkness.

But the dismal weather wasn't stopping the volunteers who'd turned out. With the river depth edging precariously close to danger levels after three days of steady rain, it seemed everyone in town had shown up to help with the hard, messy work of sandbagging.

There was more than enough material on hand for a series of articles.

However, after interviewing a number of volunteers as well as National Guard and Red Cross spokespeople, he was ready to call it a night.

Zach drained his cup, turned to toss it into a trash container—and collided with a passing volunteer.

His hand shot out to steady the middle-aged guy, who was wearing horn-rimmed glasses. "Sorry about that."

The man waved aside the apology. "Don't give it a second thought. I'm sure it was my fault. These glasses are so fogged up and wet I can hardly see where I'm going." He took them off and wiped them with a handkerchief, then put them on and flashed a wry grin. “That’ll help—for about two minutes.”

“I hear you. It’s a nasty night.”

“Yes, it is. I hope we can keep up with the river.” He held out his hand. “Phil Carr. English teacher at the high school.”

Zach returned his firm grip and introduced himself.

“Oh, yes. Mark Holt mentioned you to me. He lives on my street.” Phil hesitated a moment. “To tell you the truth, I’m glad I ran into you.”

“Why is that?”

“I hope you won’t think this is too much of an imposition, and I understand if you’re too busy to take this on, but I teach composition and it would be a treat to have a reporter from St. Louis talk to one of my classes. Do you think you might be able to spare an hour or two before you go back?”

Zach brushed his thumb over his empty cup.

It had been years since he’d been in a classroom, and his skills were probably rusty. But it might be fun.

“I’d be happy to. I actually double-majored in college—journalism and education—because I couldn’t make up my mind between the two. But a newspaper offer came through first when I graduated, so that sealed my fate.”

“Wonderful. Would you mind sharing your contact information with me?” Phil pulled out his phone and typed in the number as Zach recited it. “Thanks again. The kids will enjoy this.” He slipped his cell back in this pocket. “Now it’s back to the trenches for me.” With a wave, he strode off.

Zach watched him leave, then surveyed the scene again.

The ranks were thinning, but that wasn’t a surprise. It was nine o’clock, after all. Most of these people had put in a full day at work and would have to do the same tomorrow.

It was amazing they’d showed up at all. Especially since the homes and businesses of the vast majority of the volunteers weren't threatened by the flood.

Yet here they were, lending a hand even under these miserable conditions, while he went back to his warm, dry motel room.

A twinge of guilt nipped at him, but he quashed it. He'd been working long hours too. And he had notes to review from today's interviews before he called it a night.

Zach stepped out from under the tent and made his way past the line of sandbaggers, shivering despite his sheepskin-lined jacket. The cold rain was working its way down his neck, and his boots made loud sucking sounds as he trudged through the mud.

The tired faces of the volunteers registered in his peripheral vision as he passed, and his admiration swelled yet again. Sandbagging was backbreaking work, as he'd learned in the past couple of days, yet people of all ages and genders were here to help, from high-schoolers to grandfathers to—

Zach halted. Stared at a slight figure up ahead in one of the sandbag lines.

Unless his eyes were deceiving him, that was—

"Zach!"

At the summons, Zach tore his gaze away from the volunteer and swiveled around. "Hi, Mark."

"Working late?"

"Yes. But I'm about to call it a night." He motioned to the figure he'd spotted up ahead. "Tell me I'm wrong, but is that—"

"Rebecca?" Mark finished for him. "Yeah. She's been helping every spare minute since the call went out for sandbaggers. I've been trying to convince her to go home for the past hour. I even offered her a ride, but she said she wanted to stay."

"How long has she been here?"

"I don't know when she arrived, but she was here when I showed up three hours ago."

Three hours?

Zach's stomach clenched. "She must be frozen—and exhausted."

"I agree. Why don't *you* try to convince her to leave? Maybe you'll have better luck than I did." He waved to a figure in the distance. "Hey, Joe! Wait up. Zach, I'll see you later."

As Mark disappeared into the darkness, Zach refocused on Rebecca.

Her motions were robotlike, as if she was operating on pure adrenaline. Which was probably the case. How in the world had she lasted for more than three hours? Her slender build and delicate bone structure didn't lend themselves to this kind of heavy work. Couldn't whoever was in charge see that?

Mashing his lips together, he strode over and laid his hand on her shoulder.

She jerked toward him, her eyes dull with fatigue. "Zach? What are you doing here?"

One sweep of her face confirmed his assumption.

She was exhausted.

"Zach?" She frowned at him.

"Hang on a sec." He glanced around and signaled to a passing National Guard member toting a clipboard. When the man detoured their direction, Zach motioned toward Rebecca. "Do you have someone who can fill in here? She's about ready to fold."

The man gave Rebecca a quick appraisal and nodded. "No problem." He turned, scanned the group on the sidelines, and waved over another Guard member. "Dave, take over here for a while."

"Wait. What's going on?" Rebecca held her ground as Zach tried to urge her away from the sandbag line.

"You need a break."

Her eyes narrowed and she squared her shoulders. "Excuse me?"

Uh-oh.

Too heavy-handed.

Better backtrack. Try logic. Cajole her. Or better yet…blame his friend.

"Mark said he tried to convince you to call it a night an hour ago and you refused. I decided to see if I'd have any better luck."

"You didn't try to convince me. You just took over."

He rubbed the back of his neck.

Yeah, he had.

"I'm sorry. But I can see you're beat. If you keep at this, you're going to get sick—or hurt. And who will run your restaurant if that happens?"

She caught her lower lip between her teeth. "What time is it?"

"After nine."

Her eyes rounded. "I didn't realize it was that late." A gust of wind tugged at several strands of wet hair that had escaped from her French twist and whipped them across her face. As a shudder rippled through her, she reached up to tuck them into the band of her earmuffs.

Before she could lower her hand he grasped it, stripped off her wet glove, and cocooned her icy fingers between his palms. "Mark says you've been out here three hours or more." He gentled his voice. "You're chilled to the bone, you're wet, and you're exhausted. You need to go home where it's warm and dry and get some rest."

She took a shaky breath, the resolve in her eyes wavering. Then her shoulders sagged. "I guess you're right. I had a busy day at the restaurant, and I have to be up at six tomorrow." She scanned the area. "I got a ride here with a neighbor, but she left a while ago. Mark said he'd give me a lift, though. I just need to find him."

"I'll be happy to take you home. I was leaving anyway, and in a town this size your place can't be far out of my way. Besides, you gave me a ride once, so let me return the favor." He propped up the corners of his mouth.

She hesitated...but only for a heartbeat. "Okay. Thanks."

The tension in his shoulders eased, and he motioned toward the next street. "I'm about a block away."

The dismay on her face came and went so fast he almost missed it, but that fleeting glimpse was clear evidence that she was about to drop and didn't relish a hike.

He stayed close as they started their trek, her stiff, dragging gait screaming fatigue, every step an obvious effort for her.

Halfway to the car she stumbled, and he grabbed her arm. "Are you okay?"

"Yes. Fine."

But she wasn't.

So he maintained his grip on her as they continued.

She didn't protest.

When they reached his car he pulled open the passenger door and urged her inside. "Go ahead and get in, out of the wind."

"No." She held back. "My clothes are wet and muddy. I'll m-mess up your c-car." Her teeth were chattering so hard she could barely get the words out.

"My car will survive." He tried again to ease her in.

She continued to resist. "Do you have a blanket or a towel in the trunk that I can sit on?"

He blew out a breath.

The last thing he cared about at the moment was dirt on the upholstery. After all his car had been through in the past ten days, a few more smudges weren't going to hurt anything.

Rather than waste time arguing, however, he circled around to the back of the car and rummaged through the trunk for the rug he kept on hand in case he had to change a tire.

Only after he laid it over the passenger seat did Rebecca finally slide into the car. Although collapse was a more apt description. She was all-in.

He shut the door behind her, strode around to the driver's side, and started the engine.

During the short trip, she spoke only to give him directions. And every word seemed to require a supreme effort.

When he pulled up in front of her building, she reached for the door handle. "Thank you for the l-lift." Even though he'd cranked the heat up to high, her teeth were still chattering.

No way was he dumping her on the sidewalk.

"I'll walk you to your door."

Without giving her a chance to protest, he exited the car.

She was already out of the car when he reached her, but she didn't object when he took her arm again for the short walk up the path to her duplex.

Which could only mean one thing.

Her legs were so shaky and tired she didn't trust them to carry her the short distance.

When they reached her small porch, he angled his body to protect her from the wind as she dug through her pocket for her key.

But once she had it in hand, she fumbled her attempt to insert it in the lock. No doubt because her fingers were still numb from hours of being cold and wet.

A moment later it clattered to the concrete.

She started to bend down, but Zach restrained her. "I'll get it."

After scooping it up, he reached past her to insert it in the lock. Froze at her sharp intake of breath. "Are you all right?" He searched her face, which was mere inches away.

She gave a stiff nod and wrapped her arms tight around her body in a protective, keep-out gesture.

But her eyes sent a different message. Filled with an almost palpable longing, they issued a subliminal invitation he'd accept in a heartbeat with any other woman.

But not with Rebecca.

Because under the yearning there was a hint of fear.

Why?

That was a question without an answer. Or at least not one he was going to get tonight.

All he could do was hope that in time he could prove he was worthy of her confidence and she'd share the story behind that odd combination of emotions in her eyes.

So instead of tasting her lips, he slowly reached over and laid his hand against her cheek, brushing his thumb gently over her soft, silky skin. "Take a hot bath, okay? And get some rest." His words came out as rough as coarse gravel.

Her lips parted a hair as her gaze dropped to his mouth. Then it snapped back up as she nodded.

He let his hand drop from her cheek and took a step back. "Good night."

"G-good night. And thank you."

"It was my pleasure."

Get out of here, Wright.

Replaying that message in his mind, he shoved his hands into the pockets of his jacket and strode into the cold rain.

Before his shaky self-control evaporated.

* * *

Oh, mercy.

Heart thumping, Rebecca leaned back against the front door, legs trembling, body quivering.

And not just because she was exhausted.

Zach Wright was as much to blame for her wobbly condition as the hours she'd put in filling and hefting sandbags.

Because despite her lack of experience with men, the look in his eyes moments ago as the heady scent of his appealing after-shave invaded her pores had been clear.

He'd wanted to kiss her.

And she'd wanted him to—which was even more disturbing.

She pushed away from the door, tugged off her earmuffs, and shed her damp coat.

It was late. She ought to go to bed and forget about tonight's encounter with the St. Louis reporter.

But despite her fatigue, sleep was going to be elusive.

She trudged into the kitchen and set about brewing a cup of herbal tea. That, plus a soak in a hot tub, might soothe her aching muscles and set the stage for slumber.

Ten minutes later, as she sank beneath the lavender-scented water and sipped her tea, her body did begin to relax.

Her mind?

Different story.

After ten minutes of trying to convince it to settle down, she gave up. May as well go to bed and hope her body was tired enough to overrule her hyper-charged brain.

And fatigue might have trumped adrenaline—if her cell

hadn't pinged with an incoming text as she was climbing into bed.

She picked it up from her nightstand. Did a double take.

Zach was texting her?

How had he gotten her number?

Fingertips vibrating, she clicked on the text.

Sorry to bother you again tonight, Rebecca. Mark gave me your number. I found your wallet in my car when I got back to the motel. I didn't want to call in case you were already asleep, but I didn't want you to worry if you were still up and realized it was missing. I'll drop it by the restaurant to-morrow. If you're reading this tonight, sweet dreams.

She pressed the phone to her chest. Took a deep breath.

The message didn't require a response tonight. And it would be safer to silence her phone for the night and send a quick thank-you tomorrow. There was no need to engage in conversation.

Instead, her fingers started typing a response. A foolish move for a women who prided herself on being smart and protecting her heart, but her brain didn't seem to be firing on all cylinders at this point.

Still up. Hadn't noticed the missing wallet. Thank you for letting me know.

If your driver's license is in there, I can drop it at your apartment early.

No need. It's a short drive to the restaurant, and I don't plan to break any traffic laws. ☺

If I come after the lunch rush, would you have a cup of coffee with me?

She hesitated.

Saying no after his help tonight would be rude, but even though he'd suggested they be friends what she'd seen in his eyes tonight was closer to attraction than friendship. He'd left without trying to steal the kiss she'd lay odds had been on his mind, but what if he realized she was attracted to him too? What would she do if he—

No.

She didn't have to wonder what she'd do. She knew.

Her stomach knotted and she closed her eyes.

She'd freak out. Embarrass both of them. Maybe even make him angry. Who knew how he'd react? But based on past experience, it wouldn't be pretty.

So no matter how tempted she was to cave if he broached the subject of dating again, she'd have to muster all her resolve and—

Her phone pinged again.

You still there?

She opened her eyes. Started typing.

No promises. It can be crazy at the restaurant.

I'll take my chances. See you then.

She switched the phone to silent and set it on the nightstand with shaky fingers.

All she had to do was keep avoiding him and buying herself time. Ste. Genevieve was only a temporary beat for him, after all. Once the flood situation ebbed, he'd go back to the lights and excitement and action of the bit city and forget all about the restaurant owner who'd caught his fancy during his brief stay in small-town America. Then she'd be safe.

Until he was gone, however, she had to stay on high alert.

Otherwise, there was a very real danger he could undermine her resolve to keep him at arm's length…which would only lead to disaster.

* * *

Zach typed the final line of his story, leaned back, and massaged his temple.

It had been a long, cold, wet night, and he was operating on fumes.

But in spite of his fatigue, he'd been too wired to sleep after that sizzling moment on Rebecca's porch.

So even though the article wasn't due until early afternoon tomorrow, he'd soldiered on. Besides, he'd always done his best writing at night.

And this piece was one of his better efforts.

He scrolled back to the beginning and read through it again. Made a few edits. Nodded.

It uplifted. It reaffirmed. It found goodness even in the midst of chaos and tragedy.

It was the kind of story Josef would like.

As an image of his best friend flashed through his mind, Zach took a slow breath.

He could use a dose of Josef's optimism about now. His journalism school classmate's passion for tilting at windmills never wavered, no matter the setbacks or challenges he faced.

Zach pushed back his chair. Stood. Began to pace.

When exactly has his own idealism given way to cynicism?

Perhaps it had been three years ago, during his coverage of the story on fraud and bribery in the building industry that blew up in his face thanks to a well-crafted smear campaign that dinged the credibility of his reporting with readers, if not with his boss. Or it could have been the piece he'd done on teenage prostitution last year, when he'd spent too many depressing nights on the streets with kids who should have been at pep rallies or studying for algebra exams instead of hawking their bodies.

The corruption story he'd been told to put on hold was just another nail in the coffin of his once-strong conviction that his writing could right wrongs and make the world a better place.

He wiped a hand down his face.

Maybe his problem was burnout, as Ted had hinted. Maybe he did need a break.

Yet not everyone burned out.

Josef certainly hadn't.

At the window, Zach paused, leaned against the frame, and stared into the darkness outside.

Even now, Josef was fighting the good fight, as he called it, back in Eastern Europe, trying to make his country safe and free. A formidable task if ever there was one. Yet his commitment had never faltered.

Zach filled his lungs and propped his shoulder against the edge of the window as the headlights of a passing car briefly penetrated the gloom outside.

A Josef fix was exactly what he needed to counter his growing disillusionment.

But that wasn't going to happen anytime soon. It had been almost seven years since they'd had an in-person visit, and then only because Josef had agreed to bring his wife to St. Louis for the birth of their daughter after health complications arose that were best addressed at a big-city medical facility.

All at once, a conversation he'd had with his friend during their six-week stay, when he'd asked how Josef dealt with discouragement, replayed in his mind.

"But, Zachary, I don't get discouraged." Josef seemed surprised by the question.

"How can you not? Are conditions any better in your country now than when you started? Have you seen any progress?"

"I have not seen much visible evidence of progress, no. But we are making inroads."

"How do you know?"

"Faith. In your country, you expect things to get better like this." Josef snapped his fingers. "Patience is not a virtue in America. But in my country, we are used to waiting."

"For how long?"

Josef shrugged. "Change is slow. But more and more people are on our side, Zachary, and one day there will be freedom for all. Maybe not in my lifetime. But still, I must do my part. Because I believe that everything we do makes a difference, my friend. That no good work is ever lost. It is just that sometimes we do not see the results at once."

Shoulders slumping, Zach turned away from the darkness. Wandered back to his laptop.

Much as he'd like to believe what Josef had said was true,

evidence suggested otherwise.

As far as he could see, all his years of personal sacrifice while questing for truth and right hadn't made one bit of difference in the human condition. If anything, crime was worse now than it had been when he was an eager cub reporter, determined to change the world.

Surely Josef could see that too.

Or was it possible that having someone to love made a difference in your outlook?

Maybe.

But journalism had been the only passion in his life, and it had left him little time for anything—or anyone—else.

Except Josef had found time for love, and he was just as committed to his work. Maybe more so, given the unsettled political conditions in his country that were becoming more volatile each day.

Zach sank back into his chair. Furrowed his brow.

Yet in spite of those precarious conditions, he'd had the courage to create a family in the midst of chaos, to share his life with people he loved, viewing his family as an anchor and source of strength, not a distraction.

Maybe that was why he hadn't burned out. In the atmosphere of love and goodness and faith that pervaded his home, perhaps Josef found strength and hope and inspiration.

Zach lifted his hand. Touched the pewter ring that had been Josef's parting gift to him, inscribed with two simple words. Friends. Always.

And they would be.

Even if it had to be long-distance.

In fact, he ought to send Josef a note. It had been two weeks since they'd been in touch. A longer stretch than usual.

He opened his email, only to find a new message from Josef, sent hours ago while he'd been out covering the flood story.

His mouth flexed.

Great minds and all that.

But when he opened the email and scanned the message, his lips flatlined.

> Things are not very good for us right now, Zachary. Katrina had a miscarriage and is very ill. I wish we could be in St. Louis with good Dr. Anderson, who took such fine care of her when Isabel was born. But we must stay here and pray that God will watch over us.
>
> I cannot write much now, my friend. It is not safe here at the newspaper office. We will be moving again soon. It seems that our talk of freedom is causing much distress to the powers that be. Yet still we persevere, for the torch must be carried.
>
> I hope, Zachary, that all is well with you. I think often of our days at Mizzou. It was a happy time, was it not? So much hope and enthusiasm and optimism. We were going to change the world, you and I. Remember? And we are, you know. It is just slow work. But we must carry on.
>
> I will write again when I can. Now I must return to Katrina, who fills my life with such joy.

I pray she will be well again soon. And I pray also that peace will soon return to our troubled country.

Know that you are always in our thoughts and prayers.

Zach closed his eyes.

Bad news all around.

Katrina no doubt needed more medical assistance than she was getting. And Josef's references to danger were deeply disturbing. It was obvious his powerful, persuasive writing was attracting more and more attention from opposing factions. And caution wasn't in Josef's nature, not when he felt he was doing the right thing.

If only there was some way he could help his friend.

Zach swiveled toward the window and stared again into the darkness.

How could he honor the promise he and Josef had made to each other long ago, to help if ever the other needed assistance?

Only prayer came to mind.

And though his faith had taken a hit in recent years from too much exposure to man's inhumanity to man, on this cold, rainy night he took a moment to send a plea heavenward for protection for Josef and Katrina and Isabel.

For in the perilous environment in which the three of them lived, only a higher power would be able to keep them safe.

4

Rebecca sighed and swiped the back of her hand across her forehead.

Man, was she beat.

A long day at the restaurant, followed by hours of sandbagging, were taking a toll. And there was no end in sight weatherwise, according to the meteorologists. They continued to predict severe and widespread flooding.

All she could do was pray it wouldn't be as bad as the last flood, before she'd moved here. Families homeless, businesses ruined, hundreds of lives turned upside down—she shook her head. This town didn't need another catastrophe like that.

She glanced at her watch. Groaned.

Ten at night wasn't an ideal time to be getting ready for the bridal shower booked for tomorrow, but sandbagging had taken precedence earlier in the evening.

She dipped a spoon into the potato leek soup.

Perfect consistency.

Now she could move on to the last items on her to-do list. And if she was lucky, she'd get home before midnight.

As she walked toward the refrigerator, a knock sounded on the kitchen door that opened to the back alley behind the restaurant.

She froze.

Who in the world could be here at this hour? No delivery people, that was for sure.

She crossed to the other side of the kitchen, leaving the chain in place as she opened the door an inch or two and peered into the rainy darkness. Did a double take.

Zach lifted a hand in greeting. "Hi. Sorry if I startled you."

It took her a second to regroup. "What are you doing here?"

"I was driving by the alley and saw light spilling from your window. I wanted to make sure everything was okay."

"Everything's fine. I was, uh, just catching up on a few things." But as long as he was here, she ought to apologize for avoiding him when he'd dropped off her wallet—even if she had a legitimate excuse. "Listen, I'm sorry I couldn't join you for coffee earlier in the week. Usually the pace slows after the lunch rush, but a customer cornered me to talk about a birthday luncheon for her husband."

"No worries. Business comes first." He turned up his collar and dug his hands into the pockets of his coat.

"Why are you out so late?"

"After I finished work for the day, I pitched in for a while with the sandbagging. Can't you tell?" He hitched up one corner of his mouth and waved a hand over his mud-splattered jeans. "If some kind soul hadn't loaned me a slicker, I'd look much worse than this."

Rebecca gave him a head-to-toe. What he looked was cold and wet and—as her gaze returned to his face—tired. Lines fanned from the corners of his eyes, furrows dented his brow, and brackets framed his mouth. "Do you think you should be sandbagging? It's been less than two weeks since you had the concussion."

"I feel fine. Or I did until a little while ago, when I started to get a headache. Sleep and food should take care of that. I'm going to grab a bite somewhere and call it a night." He offered her a strained smile. "I'll see you around." He started to turn away.

"Zach…wait." The words were out before she could stop them. But she couldn't let him walk away when he was cold and hungry and in pain. Not after he'd taken her home the night he'd found her sandbagging and spent hours this evening doing that heavy lifting himself.

He angled back, eyebrows raised.

"Didn't you have dinner?"

"No. I tend to forget about food when I'm working on a story."

She swallowed. "I don't have much hearty fare on hand, but would you like a bowl of soup?"

His forehead puckered. "I wasn't angling for a meal, Rebecca. I just wanted to make sure you were okay."

"I appreciate that. And I have plenty of soup."

He hesitated. "I have to admit that aroma is hard to resist."

"I'll take that as a yes." She slid the chain free, then swung the door open. "Come on in." After he entered, she closed the door again and slid the chain back in place. "If you've been sandbagging, you're probably cold and—" The words died in her throat as he pulled off his cap, revealing the gash line near his hairline. It was obvious the staples had only recently been removed, the small punctures on either side of the mending laceration still bright and—

"It's not as bad as it looks."

At Zach's amused comment, she yanked her gaze away from the cut. "Sorry. I didn't mean to stare."

"No problem. I stared at it too when I first saw it. So much for any hopes I might have harbored of a career in modeling." He grinned.

The scar didn't mar his rugged appeal one iota as far as she was concerned, but a less personal comment would suffice. "It will fade in time. Why don't you sit on a stool at the island workspace while I get the soup?"

She crossed to the stove and ladled a generous serving into a bowl, then added a couple of pieces of homemade bread and some butter before setting the food in front of him.

"Thank you. This is a godsend. But what are *you* doing here at this hour?" He dived into the soup.

"Playing catch-up. Frances has the flu, so I'm shorthanded. And I have a special event tomorrow, which is extra work."

"Are you still sandbagging?"

"Of course."

His brow pinched. "You're going to wear yourself out."

"I can't sit on the sidelines when there's an emergency."

"But that kind of heavy physical work is hard. Especially for someone with your…of your stature."

The care and concern in his eyes sent a tingle of warmth rippling through her. "I can manage. It takes more strength and stamina to be a chef than you might think. Besides, every pair of hands helps."

"But do you have to go every night, after putting in a full day here?"

"Yes. These are my friends and neighbors. This is how life works in a small town. We help each other."

"Isn't there some other way you could help that isn't as physically taxing?"

She shrugged. "Sandbagging is where the hands are needed."

He ate in silence for a couple of minutes while she withdrew a bowl of crab salad and some Belgian endive from the fridge.

"You look like you have more chores on your to-do list for tonight." He buttered a piece of bread.

"Not too many."

"I'll tell you what…after I finish my soup, put me to work. I'm not much of a cook, but I can do simple stuff in the kitchen. That way you can get out of here sooner."

She stared at him. "I couldn't ask you to pitch in here. You're tired too, and you said you have a headache."

"It's much better now. Your soup worked magic. Come on, give me a chance. I promise I won't do anything to poison your customers."

A little trill rippled down her spine when he winked at her, practicality warring with nervousness as she picked up a stray piece of leek from the stainless steel countertop.

If she let him help, she could get out of here faster and fall into bed sooner—assuming she didn't become all thumbs and start dropping things.

Because the electricity thrumming through the air was potent…and potentially disruptive.

Maybe exhaustion was sapping her good sense, but she motioned to the bowl of crab salad and Belgian endive. "I need the endive leaves filled, if you want to tackle that."

"Sure. If you'll demonstrate the technique." He moved closer and watched her do a couple, then tugged the spoon from her fingers. "I can handle that. Go ahead and do whatever else needs to be done."

"Let me know if you want to call it quits."

"I'm not a quitter." His gaze fastened onto hers.

Oh, boy.

There was more to that comment than Belgian endive.

Had someone just turned up the heat in here?

"Um…I'll just be over there." She gave a vague wave toward the farthest end of the farthest counter, then hurried to it and tried to focus on chopping the green part of the leek for the soup garnish.

But she couldn't resist stealing occasional glances at Zach while she worked.

His brow was knitted in concentration, but he was doing well. Filling the endive just as she'd shown him, with the correct amount of salad.

She homed in on his fingers. They were strong, nimble, capable, confident. The kind that would know just how to touch a woman and—

"Am I doing it right?"

Drat.

He'd caught her staring.

She flashed him a quick look, then turned away to hide her telltale blush. "Yes. Fine." *Change the subject, Rebecca.* "Um…I heard you lectured at the high school yesterday."

If he noticed she was a bit breathless, he made no comment. "I'd say the grapevine is alive and well in Ste. Genevieve."

"It's a small town. Word travels fast. Phil told Mark, and Mark told me. Being in a classroom must have been quite a switch for you."

"It's been a while, but I double-majored in journalism and education in college, so I've logged a fair number of classroom hours. When I got offered a newspaper job after graduation, though, my teaching career ended before it began."

"What's your main job at the paper?"

"I did a little bit of everything in the beginning, but now my usual beat is investigative reporting."

She arched her eyebrows at him. "The flood coverage doesn't seem to fall into that category."

For an infinitesimal moment, he froze. Then he resumed his

methodical work. "It doesn't. This is out of pattern for me."

Hmm.

There must be a story there.

"May I ask what prompted such a different kind of assignment?"

He scooped up more crab salad and carefully fitted it into the endive, faint furrows creasing his brow. "I've been working on a series on corruption in city government, and a couple of the people implicated got wind of it. They claimed I was using falsified documents as a basis for my coverage and threatened to sue the paper if the series ran. So the publisher put a hold on the story while they figure out how to proceed and sent me off to Ste. Genevieve for the duration."

"That must have been tough to deal with."

"Yeah. It's been a real downer. This isn't the first time I've gotten burned, but it rankled more than usual. And I wasn't shy about expressing my displeasure to my editor. I think that's why he decided I needed a break from investigative work. In hindsight, I think he was right. In fact, I may need a break not just from investigative work, but from reporting in general."

"Could you take some time off?"

"I think so. I have a ton of vacation stockpiled. In fact, I laid the groundwork with my editor yesterday. Being in the classroom with those kids earlier in the week reminded me that there are a lot of ways to make a difference in the world. Maybe I need to explore a few new ones."

As an idea began to form in her mind, Rebecca continued to dice the ham for the quiche that would be served at the shower. "Did you know that Phil Carr hurt his back sandbagging last night?"

Zach looked over. "No. I'm sorry to hear that."

"Mark told me earlier tonight, when I grabbed a cup of coffee in the volunteers' tent. It sounds like he'll be out of commission for the rest of the semester. They'll be looking for a replacement to come in after spring break. And now that the floodwaters appear to be on the verge of cresting, your assignment here should be winding down soon. If you're serious about taking a break, that might be a good change of pace."

"They may already have a substitute in mind."

"I don't think so." She dumped the ham cubes into a bowl. "It's short notice, and they'll need someone for eight weeks. Of course, teaching isn't as exciting as the type of work you're used to doing."

"I was never in it for the excitement. I did it because I thought I could make a difference, change the world for the better." He sent her a rueful smile. "I was idealistic back in the day."

"There's nothing wrong with idealism."

"Maybe not. But reality has a way of making you jaded. Look what happened to Don Quixote."

Rebecca frowned as she slid the ham into the commercial fridge. "Despite the depressing ending of that story, I believe everything we do makes a difference, even if we don't see the results right away. I don't think good work is ever lost." At Zach's startled look, she frowned. "What?"

"I have a reporter friend from Eastern Europe who said almost the same thing once. Despite the chaos in his country, and the setbacks and lack of visible progress, Josef still believes his efforts to build a free and just society are making a difference."

"He sounds like a man of principle and deep faith."

"He is, which always amazes me. I see very little evidence of God on *my* beat, and he has to see even less in his world."

She offered him a tiny smile. "That's why it's called faith."

"I guess." He reached for a towel and wiped his hands, then stood and rolled down his sleeves. "Where do you want this?" He picked up the tray of endive.

"In here." She opened the refrigerator door again. "Top shelf."

"Are you about ready to call it a night?"

Yes, she was. There were a couple more minor chores on her list, but they could wait until tomorrow. Exhaustion was making her bleary-eyed. "More than. I just need to turn out the lights."

He slid the tray in while she held the door open.

Once the endive was stowed, she slipped off her apron and hung it on a hook. "Thanks again for lending a hand tonight. Now go home and get some rest."

"I'll walk you to your car first."

"I'm parked right by the door."

"I'd feel better if I see you to your car."

She could protest—but the set of his jaw suggested he'd dig in his heels and she was too tired to argue. "Okay. Give me a minute."

It took less than that, and as they exited she nodded toward her older-model compact car parked a few yards away. "See? I'm right over there."

He didn't comment. Just fell in beside her as she walked toward it, dug her keys out of her purse, and hit auto-lock.

When they reached the driver's side he turned to her, his face shadowed and unreadable in the dim light. "You know I'd still like to take you out."

They were back to that.

"I thought we'd agreed to just be friends."

"A concession made on the fly. I've tried to stick to it, but it's not working."

She squeezed the strap of her shoulder purse. "I don't date, Zach. I told you that."

"I know. But you didn't tell me why."

"It's a long story."

"Stories are my business. And I'm a good listener."

She expelled an unsteady breath. "It's late, and we're both tired."

A beat passed. "That's true." But he didn't seem in any hurry to leave. "Would you go out with me if I promise to be on my best behavior?"

"What would be the point?"

"I'm hoping if you get to know me better you'll change your mind about dating me."

At least he was honest and straightforward.

"You'd be playing very long odds. Why waste your time?"

"Let's just say I'm an eternal optimist."

"That's not what you said earlier about your work."

"This isn't work-related." He lifted his shoulders, lips flexing. "I guess I'm still idealistic in my personal life. Josef and his wife, Katrina, inspire me. Will you do me a favor and think about a no-obligations, no-expectations, hands-free date?"

She should say no.

But wouldn't it be lovely to spend a stress-free evening with a handsome, charming man who didn't expect a payoff?

The least she could do was promise to consider it. What would be the harm in that?

"I'll think about it."

The surge of warmth in his eyes chased away the chill in the damp air. "That's the best news I've had all day. And I'll think about the news you passed on about the teaching slot. A change of pace is starting to sound more and more appealing." He opened the car door. "Drive safe."

"I will." She slid behind the wheel.

But as she pulled out of her parking spot and glanced in her rearview mirror to find him watching her, she admitted the truth.

He'd opened another door tonight besides the one to her car. Namely, the one to her heart.

And foolish as it was to get her hopes up, perhaps she should keep an open mind as well.

After all, if Zach was willing to play by her rules and at her pace, maybe…just maybe…he might turn out to be a man she could trust with the secrets—and the heartaches—that had kept her from the happily-ever-after she'd always longed for.

5

Katrina was dead.

As Zach stared at the message in his email on Sunday night, trying to absorb the news, a shock wave rolled through him.

No.

It wasn't possible.

Yet as he read Josef's email again, the harsh reality of the words stole the breath from his lungs like a full-on body slam to the solar plexus.

> I do not know how I find the strength to write these words, my friend. Though the outside world goes on around me, my own world seems to have ended.
>
> Katrina died two days ago, Zachary. The miscarriage depleted her strength, and infection set in. She was never physically strong, as you know. But she had such inner strength that I thought her light could never be dimmed, that it would always burn brightly to light my way. Yet God has chosen to take her from me, leaving my world in darkness.

I write to you now to request a very great favor. Do you remember the promise we made many years ago, to help each other should the need ever arise? I hope that you do, my friend, because the time has come when I must make such a request. I do so with full understanding of the burden it will impose on you, and for that, I apologize.

Things are not good in my country, as you know. They are especially not good right now. I do not care much for myself, but I worry about Isabel. She is all I have left now, and I must keep her well. But that is not easy to do. It is no longer even safe for her to go out and play. There are too many random acts of violence and bombings. My work is also putting me at more risk. If something should happen to me, I do not know what would become of my precious child. I would turn to my family for help, but my mother is too old and frail to care for her, and my sister can barely put enough food on the table for her own children.

So, my friend, I ask you from my heart to take Isabel for a few weeks, until things settle down here and it is safe for her to return to me. I know it is a great favor to request, but I do not know where else to turn. There will surely be many details to work out, arrangements to make, red tape to cut through. But all our papers are in order, and I am confident that with your help, we can accomplish this and keep my Isabel safe. I will, of course, pay any expenses involved, including child care.

I will wait anxiously for your reply, Zachary. And may God be with you.

Zach expelled a breath. Wiped a hand down his face as a tsunami of emotions crashed over him. Grief. Fear. Anger. Frustration. Desperation. Love. Compassion. Confusion.

Anger rose to the top.

How could God deprive Josef, his good and faithful servant, of a cherished wife? How could he take away the mother Isabel needed? How could he reward a follower's sacrifice and fidelity with death and destruction?

It wasn't fair.

Zach fisted his hands. Acknowledged the hard truth.

Life *wasn't* fair. His work covering the darker side of human nature was proof of that.

He blinked to clear his vision. Printed out the message and reread it.

On the second pass, with a hard copy in hand, Josef's request seemed even more urgent.

But how was he supposed to handle this?

Of course he remembered their promise to each other. It was one they'd both meant with every fiber of their being during those heady years in J school that seemed a lifetime ago.

Promises made in the optimism and fervor of youth, however, weren't always easy to keep years later. Circumstances changed. Life became more complicated.

Yet a promise was a promise. A sacred trust not to be treated lightly. If their situations were reversed, Josef wouldn't hesitate to honor his vow.

So how could he do any less for this man who was as close to him as a brother?

Zach leaned back, brain clicking into high gear.

The logistics of Josef's request could be dealt with. He had plenty of contacts from his years of reporting, colleagues all over the world who knew how to cut through red tape.

But how on earth would he cope with a six-year-old girl who had just lost her mother and was being sent far away from her beloved father and the only home she'd ever known? His experience with children would fit in the cap of a flash drive.

No answer came to mind.

And as the sleepless hours inched by, he had no clue where to find one.

* * *

Rebecca came to an abrupt halt as she rounded a bend on her favorite trail in Hawn State park. Gaped at the man who'd been dominating her dreams.

It was unusual to see *anyone* in the park on a Monday at this time of year.

So what was Zach doing here?

She gave him a once-over, keeping her distance.

He was just off the path, sitting on a large flat boulder by the stream, arms around his bent knees, his expression pensive. Odd vibes wafted from him. Sad, almost.

As she hesitated, debating whether to beat a quiet retreat, he glanced up. Did a double take.

But he recovered from his surprise faster than she had, his shock giving way to a slight smile that seemed strained. "Fancy meeting you here."

"It's my favorite place to hike." She stayed where she was.

"I can see why. It's peaceful. Contemplative." He sighed. "But the ambiance hasn't given me any clarity yet."

She inched closer, cataloguing the shadows beneath his lower lashes and the weariness in his features. "Are you thinking about the substitute teaching position?"

His face went blank for a moment before understanding dawned in his eyes. "No."

That was all he said, but somehow she knew the creased sheet of paper in his hands was the key to the tension and melancholy emanating from him.

She moistened her lips. "I don't mean to pry, but is everything okay?"

His Adam's apple bobbed. "As a matter of fact, no. I got some bad news last night. My friend Josef…his wife had complications from a miscarriage, and she…she died." His voice rasped on the last word, and his irises began to shimmer before he bowed his head.

Pressure built in Rebecca's throat, and she crossed to him. Laid a gentle hand on his shoulder. "I'm so sorry."

"Me too." He took a shaky breath. "We went to journalism school together and stayed in touch all these years despite the geographic distance between us. We're more like brothers than friends. In fact, he and Katrina asked me to be their daughter's godfather." He pulled out his wallet and flipped to a photo before handing it to her. "This picture was taken the day of Isabel's christening. They came here for a visit shortly before she was born."

Rebecca examined the shot. A younger Zach, gingerly holding a tiny bundle wrapped in white, was flanked by an attractive, delicate-looking woman and a slender, dark-haired man with compelling eyes. "They look like a nice family. You all must be close if they asked you to be the godfather."

"We are." He gazed at the picture, his eyes pools of grief. "I told them they should ask a relative, but Josef said sometimes ties of the heart are stronger than blood. And that they'd be honored if I became part of their family in this way." His voice broke, and he dipped his chin again.

To give him a moment to regain his composure, Rebecca turned her attention to the facing picture of a little girl about six years old. Clearly this was Isabel. She had her mother's long brown hair and delicate bone structure and Josef's inquiring blue eyes. But her expression was solemn, as if she'd seen too much for someone so young.

"That's Isabel."

She looked up when Zach spoke. "I can tell. I see the family resemblance. Losing her mother will be so hard on her."

"It gets worse."

Rebecca blinked. "How could it get any worse?"

In silence, Zach held out the creased sheet of paper he was holding.

She handed his wallet back and took the eight-and-a-half-by-eleven sheet.

As she read Josef's note, her heart broke. In a few brief but eloquent sentences he'd captured the love and devotion, pain and loss, desperation and fear that now consumed his life.

"Oh, Zach." She sank down on the rock beside him. "The conditions over there sound so dangerous. I can't imagine trying to deal with that on top of such grief."

"I know. If he wants to send Isabel here, it's even worse than I thought. He wouldn't go to such an extreme unless the situation was desperate."

"What are you going to do?"

He wiped a hand down his face. "I don't know. I have to find a way to help Josef, but I don't have any experience with children. Plus, I was going to approach the school about the teaching job. Except I don't know how I'd juggle that while trying to take care of Isabel." He picked up a pebble. Hurled it into the stream, frustration radiating from him. "Ste. Genevieve would be a good environment for her, though, after all the problems in her country. And it would be safe here." His shoulders slumped. "That's why I came out here today, to try to work things out in my mind."

"It's a complicated situation." To put it mildly.

"Tell me about it."

She frowned. "If you took Isabel, could you even communicate with her?"

"Yes. Josef made sure she was bilingual."

Silence fell, broken only by the trill of a cardinal as an idea began to take shape in Rebecca's mind. It wouldn't be convenient, but after hearing Josef's plight, she knew in her heart it was the right thing to do.

She angled toward Zach. "I could help you with Isabel."

His head twisted her direction, confusion clouding his eyes. "Why would you want to get involved in this?"

"Because these people need help."

"But you don't even know them."

"It doesn't matter. Need is need."

His features softened. "Kind of like an injured motorist who needed help on a foggy night not long ago. And a town that needs help staving off an impeding flood." He let out a breath, warmth softening his brown irises. "You're a remarkable woman, Rebecca Matthews."

Heat suffused her cheeks. "I just believe in following the golden rule."

"And you do it better than most." Then he shook his head. "I appreciate your offer more than I can say, but you're too busy already between running the restaurant and helping with the sandbagging. I guess I could try to find a daycare situation for her. Josef offered to pick up child-care expenses—not that I would pass all of them on."

"I'd wager he doesn't have financial resources to spare. And the flood work should be winding down." She tucked her fingers into the pockets of her jacket. "I don't have much experience with children either, so I'm not sure how much help I'll end up being, but I'm happy to volunteer my time. I bet we could pull this off if we worked together. I could watch Isabel at the restaurant while you teach—if you get the job. And I'm off on Mondays, so I'd only have her four workdays a week. I can create a corner for her in the back with plenty of things to keep her entertained."

He scrutinized her, a touch of hope and relief springing to life in his eyes. "That sounds great. But are you certain you want to get involved?"

No, she wasn't. It was a lot to take on, and it would put her in frequent contact with a man who'd made it clear he had more on his mind than friendship.

But how could she walk away from such need?

"Yes."

The tension in his face eased. "I'll owe you forever for this."

"No, you won't." She gave a definitive shake of her head. "My offer doesn't come with strings or obligations."

"We'll talk about that later. Right now, I want to text Josef and get the ball rolling."

"And I want to continue my hike." She stood.

He glanced down the deserted trail. Frowned. "I'm not sure that's safe. If you give me a few minutes, I'll go with you."

"Not necessary. I come here all the time, and I always have my pepper gel at hand." She tapped the canister on her belt. "Besides, I have a lot to think about too."

He hesitated, but after scrutinizing her for a moment he nodded. "Okay. Will you text me when you're back in your car?"

Because he cared about her and wanted to know she was safe.

Warmth spread outward from her core. "Yes. I usually hike for about an hour."

"I'll be watching for your text."

With a nod, she started down the path—and tried not to panic.

She'd taken on a lot by agreeing to help him with Isabel. In truth, it was more than a little overwhelming.

But she was in now, and no way was she backing out.

All she could do was hope for the best—and pray for guidance.

* * *

"I still can't believe how much you got done in three days."

As Rebecca spoke from the passenger seat of the van he'd borrowed from Mark, Zach flashed her a grin. "Me neither. I think an element of luck was involved."

"I'd be more inclined to attribute it to divine intervention."

"You could be right."

Because the ease with which the pieces had fallen into place was astounding.

He'd interviewed for, and been offered, the substitute teaching position. Arranged to take all eight weeks of his accumulated vacation, plus an additional four-week personal leave. Found an apartment in Ste. Genevieve and signed a short-term lease. Cut through the red tape to get Isabel's paperwork in order. And managed to connect with a foreign-correspondent friend returning from Eastern Europe, who'd agreed to courier Isabel as far as New York and then put her on a plane to St. Louis.

It was mind-blowing.

"So what's left to do before she arrives on Sunday?" Rebecca angled toward him in her seat.

"Not much. Just move some of my stuff from St. Louis tomorrow, and pick up your old bedroom furniture at your dad's house today. I appreciate that loan, by the way."

"I'm happy it will get some use. It's been sitting at my dad's house for too long gathering dust."

"And he's okay with us cleaning out one of his rooms?"

"Yes. He doesn't go in there anymore now that I've moved away. And it won't be gone that long."

Zach flipped on his blinker and passed a slow-moving pickup truck. "What did he say about you pitching in to help with Isabel?"

"He understood the need." She slanted him a look. Squirmed on the seat. "I should warn you, though. I, uh, haven't brought many men to the house through the years, even for a practical reason like this, so you may get a few questions about…us."

In other words, her father would suspect there was more to their relationship than friendship.

"What do you want me to say?"

"The same thing I did. That we're friends, and I'm helping you out in an emergency."

"Got it. But maybe he accepted your explanation at face value."

"Don't count on it."

Half an hour later, as they pulled into the driveway of the two-story frame house with a lattice-trimmed front porch, a spare, wiry man with fine gray hair came into sight from around the corner.

"He was probably in the garden, getting everything ready for spring." Rebecca opened her door and slid to the ground as Zach set the brake, then crossed to her dad, who enveloped her in a hearty hug. "It's good to see you, Dad."

"It's always good to see you too. I love it when my girl visits."

Aa Rebecca stepped back from the hug, Zach approached the duo and extended his hand after she introduced them. "Nice to meet you, Mr. Matthews."

Her father gave his fingers a firm squeeze—and gave *him* a shrewd, assessing appraisal. When he smiled, Zach had a feeling he'd just passed some sort of test. "Call me Henry. Makes me feel younger. And I'm pleased to meet you too."

"We don't want to keep you from your gardening, Dad. We'll just go up and sort things out in the room."

"The garden will always be here." He gave a dismissive wave. "But I don't have many visitors. Besides, I'd like to get to know your young man while you're here."

As Rebecca's face turned beet red, Zach tried to tame the unruly flex in his lips.

She had her father pegged.

"This isn't a social visit, Dad." Rebecca sent him a warning look. "We just want to pick up the furniture."

He ignored her back-off glower. "That won't take long. Zach

and I will have it all loaded in no time. I hoped you'd have time for a glass of lemonade and a piece of German apple spice cake. I picked one up at the bakery this morning."

Rebecca caught her lower lip between her teeth, obviously torn between wanting to visit with her father and dreading a game of dodgeball.

So he made the decision for her. "I think we can spare half an hour to visit."

She darted him a glance he couldn't interpret.

"Wonderful." Henry beamed at them. "You two go on up and decide what you want to take. I'll wash my hands at the spigot out here before I join you inside."

As they entered the house and ascended the steps, Rebecca shook her head. "Sorry about that."

"Don't be. I'm not."

She flicked him an uneasy look but made no comment.

By the time they sorted through the furnishings in her childhood bedroom and went back downstairs, Henry had their snack waiting.

After twenty minutes of lively conversation, during which Rebecca did her best to deflect questions about the two of them, she guided the exchange back to the task at hand. "We should get the car loaded, Dad."

"You always were a hard taskmaster." Henry shook his head, an affectionate twinkle in his eyes.

"We have a long drive back."

"Let's get at it, then."

Forty-five minutes later, as they stowed the last item in the van, Henry turned to Rebecca. "I know you're anxious to get back, honey, but could I ask a favor?"

"Sure." She wedged a bag containing a set of sheets between the nightstand and dresser.

"Part of the lining came loose in my only sport coat, and I'm all thumbs with a needle and thread. I was going to take it to the tailor in town, but—"

"I can mend it for you before I leave, Dad. It will only take a few minutes." She straightened up from the van. "Tailors charge an arm and a leg."

"I hoped you'd say that." His lips flexed. "I left it with your mom's sewing kit on the couch in the family room. I'll give Zach a tour of my garden while you fix it for me."

Rebecca's eyes narrowed. "There's not much to see yet in the garden, Dad. It's too early in the spring."

"You'd be surprised. The perennials are all peeking above the ground. Come on, Zach. Let's take a walk." Without waiting for a response, he strolled toward the side of the house.

Zach looked at Rebecca.

She was frowning after her father. Obviously concerned about what he might say to her young man.

But as far as Zach was concerned, this was a huge stroke of luck. Maybe in a one-on-one conversation with her dad he could find a clue about why Rebecca was so dead set against dating.

Because until he knew the why, he was working blind trying to change her mind.

He took off after her father, catching up to him in a few long strides.

"I've got thirty-two rose bushes and two nice-sized perennial beds. They're quite a sight in the summer, when everything's in full bloom." Henry led him around the side of the house and motioned to the gardens.

As Rebecca had said, however, at this point there wasn't much to see. Some flowers were poking above the ground, but nothing was blooming.

After he made a complimentary remark about the size of the garden, and Henry pointed out a few specific plants, it quickly became clear Rebecca's father had more than posies on his mind.

"Sam, my daughter-in-law, likes flowers too. She and Brad just had a little girl. Cutest little thing you ever saw. Big blue eyes and a fuzz of reddish hair. Gonna be a carrot-top like her mother, I suspect."

"So now you're a grandpa."

"Yep. Never thought it would happen, either. Brad's first wife died years ago, and I didn't think he'd remarry. You ever been married, Zach?"

Here it came.

"No. I never found the time—or the right woman."

"Seems to me you have to *make* time for some things. Course, you can't be too careful. You sure don't want to make a mistake, pick the wrong partner. That's what I always tell Rebecca. Not that she seems to be looking, though."

Zach's pulse picked up, but he kept his tone conversational. "I noticed that. Any idea why she isn't interested in marriage?"

"Nope. And it's a shame. She loves kids, and she'd make someone a fine wife. But she's always been kind of skittish around men. Like a young colt. It takes a lot of patience to make a nervous colt comfortable, and that seems to be in short supply these days."

Zach doubted Rebecca would appreciate being compared to a horse, but Henry's comment confirmed the conclusion he'd already come to. "Patience is a virtue in my book. I'm a firm believer that good things come to those who wait."

Her father gave him an appraising once-over. "Smart philosophy. And some things are worth waiting for." He nodded to the back porch, where Rebecca had emerged. "She made short work of that jacket. Let's get you two on the road."

Five minutes later, as they waved goodbye to Henry and climbed into the van for the trip home, Rebecca turned to him. "What did you two talk about in the garden?"

"Flowers."

In his peripheral vision he could see her squinting at him. "That's it?"

"He told me about his new granddaughter. He seems thrilled about that."

"He is. Anything else?"

"He talked about horses."

"Horses?" Her eyebrows shot up. "That's not a subject he's usually interested in."

"He seemed interested in them today. That's when you came out, so it was a short discussion."

"Hmm." She settled back in her seat.

For the rest of the drive, he kept the conversation focused on the logistics of preparing for Isabel's arrival.

But the puzzle that was Rebecca continued to occupy this thoughts.

Unfortunately, there were too many pieces missing to make sense of it.

And unless she supplied them, he was back to square one.

6

Rebecca scanned the crowd emerging from the plane's exit ramp, heart pounding, palms clammy.

What on earth had she gotten herself into?

Why had she thought she was capable of dealing with a child who was not only grieving, but had just been sent to live with strangers in an unfamiliar land?

She was in way over her head, and—

"This is pretty scary, isn't it?"

At Zach's comment, she tipped her chin up. He looked as nervous as she felt. "Yes."

"I think you have less to worry about than me. I have a feeling she'll bond better with a woman than with a man. And she's going to love how you decorated her room. The frilly curtains, the pink bedspread, the posters from children's movies—I would never have thought of any of that."

"I enjoyed doing it. I just hope she likes it."

"I can't imagine any little girl who wouldn't."

As the last of the passengers disembarked, a flight attendant appeared in the doorway holding the hand of a petite dark-haired child who was clutching a very raggedy Raggedy Ann doll.

Zach sucked in a breath. "We're on."

In the fifteen seconds it took to reach the pair, Rebecca studied Isabel.

The girl wore a pink sweatshirt over black leggings. Her hair was parted in the middle, pulled up and back on each side, and secured with a pink ribbon that had probably started out crisp but now lay limp and bedraggled. She was on the thin side, delicately boned, and bleary-eyed from fatigue. No surprise in light of her long trip and the emotional trauma she'd endured.

When Isabel spotted them approaching, she watched with large, solemn eyes, looking very much like a little girl who was frightened but trying hard to be brave.

When they reached her, Rebecca dropped to one knee while Zach showed the flight attendant his gate pass and ID. "Hello, Isabel. I'm Rebecca. Zach and I are so glad you came to visit us. Is this Raggedy Ann?" She reached over and touched the obviously much-loved doll.

Isabel nodded. "She's tired now." Her voice was a mere whisper.

"I'm sure she is. It was a long trip, wasn't it?"

"Yes. My papa's far away, isn't he?" A tremor ran through her words and her eyes filled with tears.

Rebecca tried to swallow past the clog in her throat as she gently smoothed some wayward strands of hair back from the wan little face. "Not if you keep him in your heart."

"That's what he said about my mama t-too." Her voice hiccupped.

"He's right. The people we love are always with us in our hearts."

Zach knelt down beside them and smiled at the waif-like child who was now in his charge. "Hi, Isabel. I'm Zach."

"I know. Papa showed me your picture. He and Mama talked about you a lot." She hugged Raggedy Ann tighter. "Thank you for all the presents you sent for my birthdays."

"It seems you like that one especially." He touched the doll.

"I do." She tilted her head and studied him. "What should I call you?"

When Zach seemed nonplussed by the question, Rebecca stepped in. "Would Uncle Zach work?"

He sent her a grateful smile, then turned his attention to the little girl. "What do you think about that, Isabel?"

"I think it's good." She gave a serious nod, then angled toward the other newcomer in her life. "But you're not my aunt, are you?"

Rebecca smiled. "No. I'm not family. But I'd like to be your friend. So why don't you call me Becca? That's what everyone did when I was growing up."

"Okay."

"Now that we have that settled, let's collect your luggage so we can all go home." Zach stood.

Rebecca rose too, folded Isabel's hand in hers, and gave it a reassuring squeeze. "That's a good idea. Raggedy Ann is tired." She arched an eyebrow at Zach. "It's past her bedtime."

He gave a slight nod and expedited the luggage collection.

By the time they made their way to the car and stowed her two suitcases, Isabel was fading fast. Hard as she tried to stay awake, her eyes kept drifting shut as Zach buckled her into the borrowed booster seat.

As he slid behind the wheel, he glanced back at his new charge. "Are you hungry, Isabel?"

"No." She yawned.

Rebecca spoke in a soft voice. "I doubt she ate much on the plane. They don't serve kid-friendly food."

"I'm open to ideas."

She lifted her tote bag from the floor, opened it, and withdrew a pack of peanut butter crackers, two chocolate chip cookies in plastic wrap, and a bottle of water. “I had a feeling she’d be too tired to stop for food.”

The look of dismay on his face tugged at her heart. “I never even thought about that.”

“That’s why two heads are better than one when rank amateurs are tackling a challenge.” She smiled at him, then angled sideways on the seat and spoke to Isabel. “I have some food for you in case you get hungry.” She handed her the crackers and cookies, opened the water, and put the bottle in the back seat cup holder.

As they drove out of the St. Louis airport and Zach pointed the car south for their trip back to Ste. Genevieve, Rebecca kept tabs on Isabel in the visor mirror.

Within ten miles, she’d eaten all the crackers, one of the cookies, and was fast asleep.

“I appreciate your offer to keep her overnight tonight, since I have an early start tomorrow.” Zach kept checking on her in the rearview mirror too. “The timing stinks. I wish I had a full day to spend with her before school starts.”

“It is what it is. Fortunately, with the restaurant closed on Mondays I have all day to get her unpacked and settled in at your place. Plus, it will give us a chance to get acquainted.” She glanced out the window and took a deep breath as she prepared to broach the idea that had come to her on the drive up. “Um…I was thinking it would be good for her to have a home-cooked meal in a family setting on her first full day in town. If you’re okay with that, I could make dinner for the three of us at your place before I go home.”

He looked at her, the temptation to accept warring with guilt in his eyes. “That would be wonderful. But I feel like I’ve imposed too much already. Besides, the last thing you need to do on your day off is cook.”

"I like to cook. And cooking for three people is different than cooking for a restaurant full of customers." But if he wasn't on board with her suggestion, she wasn't going to push it. "I understand if you want to have some bonding time alone with her tomorrow, though. It's no big—"

"Whoa. Don't rescind your offer so fast. Even though I feel selfish for accepting after all you've already done, it would be great not to have to worry about food for her after my first day subbing."

"Let's plan on it, then."

They chatted quietly about general topics for the remainder of the drive, and Zach didn't linger when he dropped them off. Isabel was out cold, and after he carried her in and set her gently on the bed, he brought in her luggage.

"If you want to pick out clothes for her for tomorrow, I'll take the rest to the apartment."

"Good idea." Rebecca chose an outfit packed at the top of the suitcase he'd brought in from the car and draped it over the back of the couch. "You should go home and get some rest. It's getting late, and you have a busy day tomorrow."

"Yeah." He massaged his forehead. "For the record, I don't know how I would have managed this without you. As it is, I still feel like I'm in over my head. I don't know a thing about little girls. And Isabel needs a mother figure right now."

"She also needs someone to stand in for Josef, and he's obviously told her a lot about you. That's why tag-teaming this was smart."

"I agree." He sighed. "Call me if anything comes up, okay?"

"I will. But I think Isabel and I will be fine."

He picked up the suitcase and crossed to the door. Paused on the threshold. "Thank you again, Rebecca."

The tenderness in his tone and in his eyes short-circuited her respiration. "You're welcome."

He hesitated for a moment, but as the air between them began to sizzle he turned abruptly and strode into the darkness toward his car.

As he pulled away a minute later, Rebecca closed the door and drew a shaky breath.

The temptation to kiss her had been written all over his face, as easy to read as a recipe for one of the Cajun dishes she sometimes prepared for a daily special at the restaurant.

And the effect had been just as spicy and hot.

Waving a hand in front of her face, she wandered back into the living room.

With the slightest bit of encouragement, he'd act on those kinds of impulses. Guaranteed. So she'd have to be careful not to give him a green light…consciously or unconsciously.

Because she couldn't risk an outcome that might be downright ugly.

* * *

When Zach opened the door to his apartment, the sound of little-girl—and big-girl—conversation drifted toward him from the kitchen.

His lips curved up.

Nice.

Far better than the quiet—and lonely—apartment he came home to each night in St. Louis.

He closed the door behind him, the savory scent of Italian spices tickling his nose. "Smells good in here."

Rebecca appeared from the kitchen as he called out, Isabel

on her heels. "Welcome home. Dinner's almost ready."

"Can I do anything to help?" He set the package he was carrying on a chair by the door.

"No, thanks. Isabel and I took care of everything, didn't we, sweetie?"

"Yes." Isabel regarded him, her expression serious. "We're having spaghetti."

"That sounds good."

"I haven't had spaghetti before."

"I told her most children like it, so she promised to give it a try." Rebecca put her arm around Isabel's thin shoulders and gave her a squeeze.

Half an hour later, after she finished every noodle on her plate, Zach smiled at her. "What did you think?"

"It was good."

"I agree. My compliments to the chef."

"Spaghetti is easy." Rebecca waved his praise aside, though a faint touch of pink on her cheeks suggested she appreciated it. "And now it's on to brownies." She stood and began clearing the table. "Isabel helped me make them."

"I didn't help very much."

"Yes, you did. And I bet Uncle Zach is going to love them."

As Rebecca carried the dinner plates to the counter, he smiled at Isabel. "There's a bag on the chair by the door with a surprise for you."

Her eyes rounded. "But it's not my birthday."

"I know. But this is a welcome-to-the-United-States present."

She slid off her chair, trotted to the chair, and returned with the bag. Pulled out a pad of drawing paper and a package of crayons.

"After we have dessert, I thought you could draw a couple of pictures for your papa of your trip and your first day here. Then I'll take pictures of your artwork and send them to him. You can work here at the table while Rebecca and I finish our coffee in the living room." He shot his child-care partner a look as she returned with a plate of brownies and set them on the table.

Her nod suggested she'd read between the lines. Understood that he wanted a chance to talk away from little ears.

"That's a great idea, sweetie." She took her seat and doled out the brownies.

"And there's more to the surprise." Zach set his phone on the table. "I texted your dad. We set up a video call for half an hour from now. So you can talk to him face-to-face after he looks at your pictures. Would you like that?"

Her face brightened. "Yes."

As soon as they finished their brownies, Rebecca cleared the table and picked up her coffee while he opened the crayons and spread them on the table. "Uncle Zach and I will move to the living room now so you have room to draw."

As she set to work, Zach followed Rebecca to the living room. Sat close beside her on the couch, angling himself away from the kitchen as he spoke in a soft voice. "How did everything go today?"

"No problems. Like I texted you this morning, she didn't move a muscle all night. We had pancakes for breakfast, went to see Ben at the diner, then came here and I got her settled in. Josef sent a number of framed family pictures, and I put them on the nightstand and dresser. I did manage to convince her to take a nap this afternoon by lying down beside her. So all in all, a smooth day. I'm not saying we won't have any glitches down the road, but the first twenty-four hours have been uneventful."

"Did she seem sad or homesick?"

"A little—but I kept her busy. That helps. So will the chance to talk to Josef tonight." Her lips curved up. "That was an inspired idea."

"I'm glad it worked out. Cell communication between here and there can be iffy, and with the conditions as bad as they are Josef won't always be in a position to do Facetime calls. But I'll arrange them as often as I can."

"Sounds like a plan. There's one other thing. I found a parcel in Isabel's suitcase, with a letter attached that was addressed to you. I put it on the top shelf of the coat closet."

"I'll check it out later."

"Now tell me about your first day at school."

He hiked up one side of his mouth. "It was a bit overwhelming, to be honest. Academia is a different world than what I'm used to. But everyone went out of their way to be helpful."

"How were the students?"

"A little wary. Scoping out the new teacher, getting the lay of the land. But they seem like good kids—in general."

"Why the qualifier?" She eyed him over the rim of her mug as she took a sip of coffee.

He frowned. "I'm teaching a creative writing class, and I had one kid who didn't turn in the homework. I mentioned his name in the teachers' lounge, and it sounds like that's not uncommon for him. Because of that, his grades are marginal. But he aces tests, so he's obviously bright. It's a shame for potential like that to be wasted."

"What's his name?"

"Pete Cramer."

She shook her heard. "I know a lot of the families here, but that doesn't ring a bell."

"From what I gathered, he comes from a broken home. I think he lives with his father, who works at the cement plant."

"Maybe no one's ever encouraged him to focus on school—or *made* him do his homework."

He arched an eyebrow, cradling his mug in his hands. "How do you make a seventeen-year-old boy do *anything*?"

"I expect it's a challenge." She cocked her head, her expression thoughtful. "Long-term, I guess it's a matter of finding a way to make him *want* to do it. But in the meantime, some discipline might do the trick."

"Not a popular word in this day and age."

"True. But being an authority figure isn't always a popularity contest. I think that even though kids may act like they resent discipline, they respect it when it's administered by someone who's genuinely concerned about them. I also think it boosts their self-esteem to know someone cares enough to take that kind of interest."

She had a point.

"I never thought of it from that perspective."

Her lips twisted. "Well, take my ideas with a grain of salt, because I don't have much experience to draw on. But it might be helpful to be firm and set the rules and expectations up front."

"I'll give that some thought."

They chatted for a few more minutes about his first day at school and logistics for Isabel going forward, until the six-year-old popped into the living room with three drawings in hand. "Is it time to call Papa yet?"

"Yes." Zach set his empty mug down. "Let me take pictures of your drawings and email them first. Then I'll make the call."

Rebecca followed them back to the kitchen, where he snapped photos of the drawings of an airplane, a bowl of spaghetti, and a pink bedroom.

"Can Becca stay while we talk to Papa?" Isabel sidled closer to her.

He'd like nothing better—but she'd gone above and beyond already today. It was only fair to give her an out, even though the thought of being one-on-one with the little girl after she left was making him more nervous than a rendezvous with a questionable source in a dicey part of town.

"She's been here all day, honey, so she may have to go home." He glanced at her but didn't try to hide the plea in his eyes.

She studied his face for a moment, then smiled at Isabel. "I can stay for a few more minutes."

After Zach placed the call and he and Rebecca had an initial exchange with Josef, she stayed in the background. So did he. Because Isabel and her papa had much to say to each other.

When the call at last began to wind down, Isabel got teary-eyed. "I don't want to say goodbye, Papa." She clutched the Raggedy Ann doll that was never far away tighter to her chest.

"I don't either, little one. But we will talk again soon. And I am sending you my love every minute of every day. Zach, Rebecca, you are still there?"

They moved back into camera range. "Yes." Zach's shoulder nudged Rebecca's as he jockeyed to get them both on screen.

"Thank you for all you are doing for my precious Isabel." The lights flickered, and when Josef reappeared his brow was furrowed. "I must go now. Please take good care of my little one."

"Count on it." Zach's voice rasped. "Stay safe, my friend."

"I have put my welfare in God's hands. And now I will say good night until we talk again."

As the screen went blank, a tear trickled down Isabel's cheek.

Now what?

He sent Rebecca a desperate look.

"Why don't we get ready for bed?" She stood and reached for Isabel's hand. "I bet you're tired."

"I…I miss my m-mama and papa." Isabel's choked voice was barely audible.

"I know. But Uncle Zach and I will take care of you until you can go home again."

"W-will you stay with me tonight?"

"I don't live here, sweetie. This is Uncle Zach's apartment. But I'll see you in the morning, when he drops you off at the restaurant on his way to school."

Rebecca handled the bedtime chores while Zach took mental notes, since he'd be on his own for the nighttime ritual from here on out.

When Isabel was at last tucked in and drifting off, he walked with Rebecca to the door. "You seem to have acquired an avid fan. I hope I'll be as lucky."

"It's probably easier for her to relate to a woman. Give her a few days to acclimate." She slipped her arm through the strap of her bag and settled it on her shoulder.

"I wish there was more I could do for her—and for Josef."

"You're doing everything you can, Zach. And the peace of mind you're giving Josef has a value beyond price. But prayer wouldn't hurt, either."

He sighed. "I haven't done much of that in the past few years."

"It's never too late to start again."

"It is tonight. I'm beat. It's been a long day—for both of us." He pulled the door open. "I'll walk you to your car."

"Not tonight. Stay close in case Isabel calls out. Besides, I'm right there." She pointed to her car just steps from his door.

He didn't argue. "I'll see you tomorrow morning, then. Are you certain seven-thirty isn't too early?"

She gave a soft laugh. "Hardly. I'm at the restaurant at the crack of dawn. And don't worry about breakfast for Isabel. I'll feed her."

How in the world had he been lucky enough to cross paths with this amazing woman? And not just because of all the help she was providing with his temporary charge.

As she looked at him, the wistful yearning that suddenly softened her features sent his pulse off the scale.

Man, it was hard to think straight when she looked at him like that, with invitation in her eyes.

It would be so easy to pull her into his arms, to let his lips say good night in a way that expressed more clearly than words both his gratitude for her support during this challenging time as well as the depth of his attraction to her.

Except Henry had been right. The key to getting past Rebecca's barriers was patience.

Before his hands did something he'd regret, he stuffed them into his pockets. "Drive safe."

She took a deep breath. Yanked her gaze away from his. "I will. It's not a long trip. Good night."

Only after she drove away did he close the door. Wander over to retrieve the package she'd found in Isabel's suitcase.

Once he had it in hand, he sat on the couch, pulled the envelope free, and slit it open.

The note inside was written in Josef's flowing hand.

Dear Zachary,

Remember how you always used to tease me

about being buttoned-up when we were in school, about never leaving any loose ends hanging? (See? I have not forgotten my American slang!) Well, I am still that way, planning ahead for all possibilities. This package is only to be opened in the event something happens to me while Isabel is in your care. Otherwise, please return it unopened when she comes home.

I will never be able to repay the great favor you and your friend, Rebecca, are doing for me. I send you my heartfelt thanks and eternal gratitude. Please know that in the weeks ahead you will both be in my prayers. And I ask that you remember me in yours as well. May God bless you and keep you.

Zach let out a slow breath. Ran his fingers over the brown paper that covered whatever Josef had sent. Who knew what was inside?

And he hoped he never found out. That the package would return with Isabel to the father who loved her with all his heart.

He stood. Stowed the parcel back in the closet. Took a deep breath.

Even though his faith had been badly dinged on the seedy beats he often worked, Josef's remained strong. As did Rebecca's.

So before he called it a night, it might not hurt to send a plea heavenward for protection for Josef—and guidance for a wayward son who was in over his head with a heartsick, homesick little girl.

7

"Pete...I'd like to see you for a minute." As Zach spoke to the tall, lanky youth, the teen paused and shot a glance at his buddies waiting in the hall.

"I have to go or I'll miss my ride." His attempt at defiance fell short.

Zach crossed to the door and closed it with a firm click. "How far away do you live?"

"About three miles."

"I'll take you home when we're finished."

"Finished with what?" The boy narrowed his eyes.

"Let me ask you something, Pete." Zach ignored the question as he propped a shoulder against the door and folded his arms. "Why did you take this class?"

He shrugged. "It sounded better than technical writing or Shakespeare."

"You did realize that in a creative writing class you'd be expected to write, didn't you?"

He stared back, expression sullen, but remained silent.

When Zach locked onto his gaze, Pete's wavered. Dropped to the floor as he shoved his hands into his pockets and shifted his weight from one foot to the other.

"I'll tell you what." Zach kept his tone conversational. "I'm new here, and as far as I'm concerned you're starting with a clean slate. You've only missed one homework assignment under my watch, and I'm going to let you make it up right now."

"Now?" Pete's chin jerked up.

"Yes. It shouldn't take you long. An hour at the most."

A beat ticked by. "What if I don't want to?"

Zach pushed away from the door and walked toward him. Halted when Pete took a startled step back—almost as if he expected to be struck.

Disturbing.

After a moment, Zach resumed his advance more slowly, maintaining a nonthreatening posture. "I think you do want to, Pete. I've heard you're an excellent student when you want to be. And Mr. Carr told me you have real talent. I'd like to see what you can do."

His eyes narrowed. "Why?"

Keeping Rebecca's counsel in mind, he chose his words with care. "I admire good writing. There's a magic in being able to put words on paper in a way that brings a story to life, whether it's an investigative article or fiction. I think it's a special gift, and people who have that gift should be encouraged to develop it. One of the best ways to do that is by writing as much as possible. So if you have the gift, I'd like to do what I can to help you hone it."

Pete's defiant posture relaxed a hair. "I'm not that good."

"Why don't you let me be the judge of that? Do you have your laptop with you?" He motioned to the teen's backpack.

"Yeah."

"Okay, have at it. I'll be up front correcting papers. No hurry." He circled the desk and sat. Thank goodness Rebecca was on board with his plan and had agreed to a late pick-up for Isabel tonight.

As the seconds ticked by, Pete remained where he was. But at last he returned to his desk, sat, and pulled out his laptop. For a full minute he stared at the screen, fingers idle. Then he leaned forward and began to type.

Zach exhaled.

This could have blown up in his face.

But Rebecca's instincts had been correct. Discipline, a clear delineation of expectations, and encouragement seemed to be the magic elixir to get results with a teen.

Zach booted up his own laptop and settled in to finish reading the homework that had been turned in on Monday, using track changes to make corrections and add both complimentary comments and constructive criticism on each paper. While many of the students were creative, there was plenty of room for improvement in terms of style, grammar, and punctuation.

After grading half a dozen papers, he paused. Tapped a finger next to the touchpad.

Had the school ever considered a journalism or editing class? Both would help students polish the basics and tighten their writing. And they shouldn't be difficult to institute. It would just require—

"I'm finished."

Zach glanced at his watch as Pete stood. Almost an hour had passed, meaning the boy had made an effort rather than blown off the assignment.

"Go ahead and email it to me while I shut down. Then I'll drive you home."

"You don't have to do that. I can hitch a ride."

"A promise is a promise."

Pete retreated to his desk, and as Zach prepared to shut his laptop down it pinged with a new email alert.

Assignment completed and turned in.

He slid his laptop into its case and rose. "How long have you lived in Ste. Genevieve, Pete?" After crossing to the door, he waited until the teen joined him before flipping off the classroom light.

"Too long."

"You don't like it here?"

"It's okay for a small town."

"You like cities better?" Zach matched his stride to Pete's as they walked down the hall.

"Yeah. I'm gonna move to Chicago or New York or LA when I get out of school. Someplace where there's more action." He sent him a sidelong look. "Are you really an investigative reporter?"

"Yes."

"Then why are you subbing in a Podunk town?"

"Serendipity, for want of a better explanation. I came here to cover the flood when my investigative assignment ran into a snag, and I realized I was ready for a break from my usual routine about the time Mr. Carr got hurt."

"Teaching must be boring after being a reporter. Covering news stories would be exciting."

Zach pushed through the door and led the way to his car. "I've seen my share of action on the paper, but to be honest a lot of it is more sleazy than exciting. And I don't find working with young people boring. Your generation is our future, and it's energizing to nurture the talent in tomorrow's leaders."

A few beats ticked by as they crossed the empty parking lot. "My dad doesn't think school is all that important. He's worked in the cement plant his whole life."

"What about your mom?"

"I don't see her much. She and Dad got divorced seven years ago and she moved out West. She didn't want to take me, so Dad got custody. But I don't think he wanted me, either." A thread of hurt wound through Pete's words under his studied indifference.

Zach hit the auto-lock button, and they both slid into the car.

No wonder the kid was having trouble in school. In fact, it was amazing he showed up at all with so little support on the home front.

He kept the conversation casual and pleasant as he drove, and when they pulled up in front of the tiny house on the outskirts of town that Pete called home, Zach turned to him. "I expect you to finish today's assignment on time."

Pete opened the door. Squinted at him. "Are you gonna make me stay late again if I don't?"

"Yes."

Pete hesitated, then slid out of the car. "Thanks for the lift."

"No problem. See you tomorrow."

As Zach pulled away from the curb, he looked in the rear-view mirror.

Pete was standing where he'd left him, staring after the car, hands in his pockets, posture slouched.

He'd tried to be firm and set the ground rules, as Rebecca had suggested, and at the same time come across as approachable and caring.

Who knew if he'd succeeded?

As Pete disappeared from view, Zach exhaled.

Teaching was complicated. The classroom work was important, but so was understanding the personal lives of the students. Because the two were inseparably entwined.

Pete seemed to have dreams of a better, different life than the one his father led. And if what the other teachers said about his intelligence was true, education could be his ticket to the larger world he craved.

The challenge was to convince him of that.

A challenge that took on heightened importance after he speed-read Pete's paper once Isabel was in bed.

Because the kid could write. Way beyond the high school level.

And if he did nothing more during his substitute teaching gig than convince Pete he had real talent and serious potential, his time here would be well spent.

* * *

"Hi, Rebecca. How's it going down in the boonies?"

At the good-natured jibe from her wise-cracking, heart-of-gold sister-in-law, Rebecca adjusted the cell against her ear, tucked her leg under her on the couch, and smiled. "Hi, Sam. I hear tell we're gonna get running water next week." She used an exaggerated country accent.

"Ha ha. But you do seem far away. We don't see enough of you."

"Right now I should think company would be the last thing you'd want. Don't you have your hands full with a little bundle of joy named Emily? How are you all doing?"

"Emily's fine. Brad and I, on the other hand, are exhausted. But we wouldn't change a thing." The muffled sound of a crying baby came over the line. "I'm being summoned, so let me cut to the chase. Do you have plans for Easter?"

"Not yet."

"You do now. Dinner at our house. Your dad is coming to visit for about a week, so he'll be here too. It will give us all a chance to catch up."

"That sounds lovely." Although she'd been toying with the idea of doing something to make the holiday special for Isabel. Zach might not have a clue how to—

"You're welcome to bring Isabel. Zach too, of course. After hearing Henry talk about him, I'm intrigued."

Uh-oh.

Hard as she'd tried in previous conversations with Sam to downplay her relationship with Isabel's temporary guardian, it sounded like her father had undermined her efforts.

"What has Dad been telling you?"

"That you brought a hot-looking guy down there to pick up the furniture for Isabel. An *interested* hot-looking guy. And he said it seemed the feeling was mutual. Of course, this is all secondhand information, you understand. We're only the brother and sister-in-law. Why should you tell us anything?"

Thank goodness they weren't on Facetime, or Sam would spot the warmth on her cheeks in a heartbeat. "I would have been glad to tell you, if there was anything to tell." She kept her tone matter-of-fact. "Zach is just an acquaintance, like I've said all along."

"Uh-huh. I'll see if I agree with Henry when you all come up. Unless you'd rather not invite him. But it seems a shame to bring Isabel and not him. He'd be all alone for the holiday."

That was true.

Which put her between a rock and a hard place.

But maybe if she mustered up every ounce of her acting skill for the few hours they'd all be together she could convince Sam and Brad—and Dad—that the two of them were only friends.

"Fine. I'll ask him. But he may not come."

"You want to place a bet on that?"

No.

Because the odds were against her.

"I'm not a gambling woman."

"Smart. Especially if you don't think you'd win. Why don't we all meet at church for the service?"

"Assuming Zach wants to come."

"He'll come."

Rebecca picked up a cushion. Hugged it against her chest. "Don't get carried away, Sam."

"From what Henry said, your friendly reporter needs that warning more than I do. Or not."

Rebecca frowned. "What does that mean?"

"It means don't be too fast to discourage him, especially if he's as nice as Henry says."

"Dad has an overactive imagination."

"Maybe. But listen, kiddo. I was into the let's-be-friends-because-nothing-else-could-ever-work-between-us mode for a long time with Brad. Thankfully your brother persevered. And now I have a wonderful husband and a beautiful daughter. All I'm saying is that if you're interested, give it a chance." Another wail sounded in the background. "Gotta run. Let me know how many to expect on Easter."

As Sam ended the call, Rebecca squeezed the cell and closed her eyes.

If only she *could* give it a chance.

But how did you control an irrational fear that could set off a full-on panic attack once it was triggered?

Maybe counseling would have been beneficial years ago. Perhaps it still could be. But it wasn't going to produce results fast enough to help her with Zach.

The other option was to tell him her story. Hope he had the patience—and a strong enough ego—to deal with her issues.

But most men didn't, as she'd learned.

So until she knew Zach better, it was safer to go on keeping her distance—no matter what Sam thought.

* * *

"Pete? I need to talk with you for a minute." Zach picked up a folder and his laptop from his desk as the students filed out of the classroom.

The teen gave him a wary look. "I turned in my homework."

"I know. I want to talk to you about something else. Go ahead and have a seat."

After a moment, he folded his lanky frame into a convenient desk and slid down into the slouch position he favored.

Zach waited until the last student exited, then shut the door and sat in the desk beside the boy. "I wanted to discuss the last piece you wrote." He opened the lid of his laptop and called it up.

Trepidation mixed with defensiveness flared in his eyes. "I had to rush. I didn't have a chance to—"

"Look at the paper, Pete." Zach angled the screen toward him.

The boy glanced at it. Blinked. Leaned closer, as if he couldn't believe his eyes. "You gave me an A?"

"You deserved it. Take a minute to read my comments." He settled back in his seat, waiting as Pete worked his way through the paper.

By the time the teen reached the last one, his jaw had slackened and his cheeks were flushed.

Zach leaned forward and tapped the screen. "That is a fine piece of work. You should be proud of it. And it confirms what Mr. Carr told me. You have talent. And I don't want to see it go to waste." He opened the folder, removed two items, and handed the first one to Pete.

"What's this?"

"Information on a national short story contest. There are monetary prizes involved, but more important, a win would be impressive on a college application. It would also give you a chance to be published." He passed over the second item. "This is a brochure about a writing camp being held in Michigan this August. It's for gifted writers, and I think you qualify. Look them both over, and we'll talk about them next week."

Pete stared at the pamphlets for a moment, and when he lifted his gaze there was a cautious hope in his eyes that transformed his expression from sullen rebelliousness to youthful optimism. "Do you really think I could do these things?"

"I wouldn't have given you the brochures if I didn't."

The boy's Adam's apple bobbed, and he averted his face. Rose. "I'll read them this weekend." His voice rasped. "Thanks." Then he fled.

Zach let him go.

A seed had been planted—and based on Pete's reaction, the ground had been receptive. It was almost as if he'd been waiting for someone to care, to take an interest, to encourage him.

Zach rose. Returned to his desk.

People's lives didn't change overnight, of course. Fifteen years of investigative reporting had taught him that. But lives *could* change, if people made an effort and learned to believe in themselves.

And Pete had just taken a step in that direction.

Only time would tell if he'd stay the course, however.

* * *

Rebecca added a dollop of whipped cream to the final piece of chocolate torte, deposited the three servings on a tray, and huffed out a breath.

This was ridiculous.

For two days she'd been dithering about how to broach the subject of Easter to Zach so he wouldn't read too much into being invited to a family event.

And for two days she'd chickened out every time she'd had an opportunity to ask him.

But now she had another chance. With him and Isabel in the restaurant, all she had to do was—

"My goodness, Rebecca, that whipped cream is going to deflate if you stand there staring at it much longer." Rose planted her hands on her hips. "Just ask the man. I guarantee he'll say yes."

Rebecca mashed her lips together.

She should never have told the sisters about the pending invitation. Wouldn't have if they hadn't caught her at a weak moment. They were already enamored with Zach, and they loved playing grandma to Isabel, who was thriving on their attention. They'd be clueless about why she was dragging her feet.

"I'll ask him for you if you want me to." Frances lifted the coffeepot and prepared to do a refill circuit.

That was the *last* thing she wanted.

Who knew what Frances would say?

"I appreciate that, but I'm going to take care of it right now. It should be quiet out there, since most of the lunch customers are gone." She lifted the tray with the desserts and pushed through the swinging door to the dining room. Paused when it closed behind her.

Zach and Isabel were having a serious exchange at a corner table, but all at once he grinned and said something that made her giggle.

At the heartening sound of childish pleasure, warmth filled Rebecca's heart.

Isabel continued to miss her home and her parents, and she often talked about them and the Facetime exchanges Zach arranged with Josef. But she seemed more comfortable now in her new environment, and was no longer as withdrawn and uncertain as she'd been in her early days in Ste. Genevieve.

Kudos to Zach for that. Surely a child was the last thing he wanted in his life at this particular time. Yet he'd honored a fifteen-year-old promise without hesitation, then reconfigured his lifestyle to accommodate Isabel. How many men would behave that unselfishly?

Not many, based on her experience.

From all indications, Zach was a man of honor and integrity and character—and Sam was right. Though her sister-in-law had toned back her usual blunt style during their last conversation, her message had come through loud and clear: If you find a keeper, don't let him get away.

And Zach seemed to be a keeper.

So maybe it was time to test the waters a bit. Stop letting fear hold her back. Take a chance.

Hoisting the tray into a more comfortable position, she started toward the duo.

Zach must have seen the movement in his peripheral vision, because he turned toward her. Sent her a smile so toasty it could melt the whipped cream on the treat she was toting.

"Are you two ready for dessert?" Her question came out a bit breathless as she dispersed the tortes and set the tray aside.

"I always like something sweet after a meal." Zach focused on her as he spoke, spiking her pulse.

"Me too. Especially chocolate cake." Isabel dived into the treat.

Zach started in on his too while Rebecca played with her fork.

"Everything okay?" He looked over at her.

No lack of perception in this man.

"Fine." She forced herself to eat a bite of cake as her pulse picked up.

Just ask him, Rebecca. Get it over with.

But her courage was deflating as fast as the whipped cream on her uneaten cake.

As Zach and Isabel had a brief exchange, she gritted her teeth.

She needed to spit out the question. Create an opening to ask it if one didn't arise. How hard could it be to—

"Isabel, the little dog from the next shop came to visit." Rose bustled over. "He's outside the back door. Do you want to say hello?"

Her eyes lit up. "Can I, Uncle Zach?"

"Sure."

She gobbled down the last couple of bites of her cake while Rebecca gave Rose a suspicious once-over.

The woman's face was the picture of innocence.

But when Frances stuck her head out of the kitchen door to watch the proceedings, Rebecca's hunch was confirmed.

The sisters had conspired to give her and Zach a few minutes alone together.

As Isabel disappeared into the back room with Rose, Rebecca took a deep breath—and took the plunge. "I don't know if you and Isabel have any plans for Easter, but I'm spending the day with my brother and sister-in-law, Brad and Sam. Dad will be there too. Sam said you'd be welcome to join us. But if you'd rather—"

"We'd love to come."

That was fast.

"Um…in case it makes a difference, we're going to meet at my brother's church for the service first. He's a minister. I know that's not part of your usual schedule."

He cocked his head. Studied her. "Are you trying to talk me out of accepting?"

"No." Not exactly. "I just want to be up-front about the plans for the day."

"Church is fine. Josef and Katrina went every Sunday, so regular attendance was part of Isabel's routine. In fact, I was going to ask if you'd mind taking her to church with you on Sundays. Rose mentioned to me once that you go every week, and I know Josef would like that. Easter Sunday may be a good time to kick that off."

"I'd be happy to take her. And you'd be welcome to join us."

"I appreciate that—and I'll think about it."

Since pushing wasn't likely to make him any more receptive to the idea, she let it pass. "So are we on for Easter?"

He smiled. "We're on. And I have a feeling it's going to be the best Easter I've had in years." He started to reach for her hand, but retracted his when Isabel pushed through the door and rejoined them, chattering about the dog.

Just as well.

While nothing would have happened if he'd taken her fingers, hand-holding led to other things.

And the results of that might not be pretty.

Rebecca took a bite of the cake she didn't want.

This was why an Easter outing could be dangerous.

All she could do was pray for guidance, keep Sam's advice in mind to give it a chance—and hope for the best.

8

Wow.

Rebecca was always beautiful. Even wet and muddy from sandbagging. But she'd outdone herself for Easter.

"Good morning."

At her soft greeting, Zach gave her a head-to-toe from the other side of her front door, pulse stuttering.

Most of the women in his acquaintance favored sophisticated, high-fashion attire. But Rebecca's outfit, which had an old-fashioned, girl-next-door charm that made him think of afternoon tea or a garden party, was uber-appealing. The full skirt flared from a cinched waist, and the pastel floral fabric echoed the spring hues of the redbuds and flowering crab trees now in bloom.

But the crowning glory—literally—was her hair.

Double wow.

Freed from the constraints of her usual French twist, the soft, unfettered waves cascaded past her shoulders, the glorious russet strands glinting in the morning sun. And her wide-brimmed straw hat, adorned with a cluster of silk flowers, was the perfect crowning touch.

Zach reached up to run a finger around his suddenly tight collar. Checked to make sure his jaw wasn't hanging open. Searched for his voice. "Good morning." The words came out scratchy, and he cleared his throat.

"You look pretty, Becca." Isabel spoke beside him.

"I'll second that."

At his husky comment, a pulse began to beat in the delicate hollow of her throat, and his eyes zoomed there like a homing pigeon on a mission.

"Look what Uncle Zach gave me!"

As Isabel held up the large, stuffed white rabbit, Rebecca sucked in a sharp breath, tore her gaze from his, and dropped down to her level. "What a nice rabbit. And don't you look pretty?"

Isabel smoothed the skirt of her sashed floral dress, touched the lace-edged ruffle at the hem, then reached up to adjust her white straw hat. "I never had a dress like this before. Or a hat, either. Thank you for helping me pick everything out."

"You're welcome, sweetie. And you're going to be the prettiest lady at church today." She gave her a hug, then stood and pulled the door wider. "Come in for a minute while I get my purse. And I think there's something on the coffee table for you." She smiled at Isabel.

Interest sparking in her eyes, she scampered into the living room. Came to an abrupt halt when a giant basket of goodies, covered with clear yellow cellophane and topped with a big lavender bow, came into sight. "Is that mine?"

"Yes. Happy Easter, sweetie."

As Isabel crossed to the table and began unwrapping the basket, Zach moved beside Rebecca. "Thank you for that."

She angled toward him. "What's Easter without a basket—or a rabbit?"

"Or an Easter bonnet. Thanks again for taking Isabel shopping for the outfit. I wouldn't have known where to start."

A soft curve bowed her lips as she regarded the little girl. "I had fun going with her."

"And she looks charming. But she won't be the prettiest lady at church. That honor will be yours."

As the words slipped from his mouth, Rebecca sent him a startled look.

Blast.

So much for pacing himself and waiting for her cues.

Better change the subject. "If you ladies are ready, we should get going. It's a long drive to St. Louis."

He kept the conversation casual during the trip, and Isabel joined in, chattering away as the miles slipped by—in marked contrast to her initial subdued reticence when she'd arrived. And the woman beside him, who'd nurtured the little girl in ways he never could have, deserved much of the credit for how well she'd adjusted to her new environment.

When they arrived at the church, he helped Isabel out of the booster seat and took her hand. Rebecca did likewise on the other side. Like they were a family.

And it felt surprisingly good, considering he'd always avoided relationships that came with even a hint of commitment, responsibility, or the constraints of a white picket fence.

But as they joined the other family groups heading toward the church under the sunny blue skies, he didn't feel one iota of panic or entrapment. Just the opposite. A sudden yearning for a family to love, like Josef had enjoyed, swept over him.

He glanced over Isabel's head at Rebecca.

As if sensing his perusal, she looked at him. Offered a tentative smile. "It's a gorgeous day, isn't it?"

"Gorgeous is the word." When a soft flush crept across her cheeks, he changed the subject. "I'm looking forward to meeting your brother and sister-in-law."

"They feel the same about you." Faint furrows dented her brow. "Just be aware that Dad's been, uh, talking to them about you. Turns out he's a closet romantic."

He hitched up one side of his mouth as they entered the church. "I kind of got that impression the day we picked up the furniture." Before she could respond to that, he tipped his head toward a pew on the left side of the church, in the back. "There's your dad."

As the crowd intensified, Rebecca released Isabel's hand and moved ahead, leaving the two of them to follow.

But he stayed close enough to hear her exchange with her family as he and Isabel approached.

"Rebecca, you look beautiful." The red-haired woman, presumably Sam, stood and gave her a hug. "Doesn't she, Henry?"

"Glowing." He rose too. "You been taking vitamins—or is there another explanation?" Henry directed a smirk his way as Zach wove around a cluster of people and guided Isabel toward Rebecca's family. Then her father nudged Sam. "What did I tell you?"

"You must be Zach." The redhead held out her hand. "I'm Sam. The outspoken sister-in-law."

Zach reached around Rebecca, who moved back into the aisle to give him better access, and returned her firm shake. "A pleasure to meet you. And this is Isabel." He drew the little girl forward and sat, putting himself on her level as she stood beside him. "Honey, this is Becca's family. Sam is married to her brother, and that's her papa." He motioned toward Henry.

Sam and Henry sat, and Henry leaned forward.

"Hi, Isabel." Henry fished in his pocket and pulled out several foil-wrapped chocolate eggs. "The Easter bunny asked me to give these to you."

She dipped her head and took them, a tiny smile curving her mouth as she spoke in a soft voice. "Thank you."

"And I have something for you back at the house." Sam winked at her.

Isabel edged closer to peek at the baby in Sam's arms, the tiny face framed by a pink bonnet edged in lace. "Is she yours?"

"Yes. Her name is Emily, and she's the reason we're sitting in the back." Sam glanced at him and Rebecca. "I hope you don't mind, but I need to be close to the exit in case she decides to exercise her vocal cords. I'm sorry to say I think she inherited her mother's big mouth."

"Can I sit next to her?" Isabel continued to stare at the baby as Emily sucked on her fist and watched the proceedings with big eyes.

"As long as Zach says it's okay. Emily does like an audience."

"Fine by me."

Sam scooted over to make room for her. "Rebecca, you can sit on the aisle. Next to Zach."

"Or I could sit next to Dad." She started to circle toward the back of the church to enter the pew from the other side, but before she could get there an older couple slid in beside Henry.

The organ began playing, and Rebecca paused.

When she looked back, Zach shrugged and motioned to the empty spot beside him. What other option did she have?

None.

So she returned, keeping as much distance between them as she could.

But Easter service attendance was high, and when the ushers shoehorned another person into the far end of the pew, everyone had to scoot over to make room—putting the two of them thigh-to-thigh.

Her breath hitched.

"Sorry for the tight quarters." He leaned close and spoke in her ear. A bit of a fib, but he could at least acknowledge her discomfort even if he didn't understand it in light of the spark of attraction that was easy to read in her eyes.

"No worries. It's always c-crowded on special days."

Rebecca's brother, Brad, entered the sanctuary, and Zach gave him a quick inspection. He was tall, late thirties or early forties, with sandy brown hair touched with silver and a toned physique. In his clerical garb, he radiated a quiet confidence and serene vibe.

For a man who no longer made regular church attendance part of his routine, Zach found the service more comforting and uplifting than he expected.

And Brad's sermon was a highlight. He was an excellent speaker, and his Easter-themed message of new life, hope, trust, and promises fulfilled resonated. Especially the conclusion.

"As you leave church today, take a moment to notice the tulips blooming on the grounds. Bulbs are a beautiful symbol of rebirth. When we place them in the ground in the fall, they appear dead. But in the spring the gentle warmth of the sun patiently coaxes them to grow and blossom.

"That's also a good analogy for a heart that longs for love, isn't it? Like the spring bulbs, it's a fragile thing that can wither away and appear to be dead. But with warmth and patient nurturing, most hearts can bloom again.

"On this Easter day, let us embrace the promise of spring. Let us find the courage to seek love if we don't have it, and the wisdom to cherish it if we do. For despite its inherent risks and heartaches, it's still the greatest gift God can bless us with in this life."

As Brad finished his sermon and moved away from the pulpit, Zach gave Rebecca a surreptitious scan.

Henry had called her a skittish colt when it came to men. Yet it was clear after watching her with Isabel that her heart was made for love, even if she shied away from dating.

Could the right man, through warmth and patient nurturing, convince her to share her love with him?

Could *he* be that man?

Maybe.

Because the notion of spending his life with the woman beside him was gaining traction with every passing day.

So maybe it was time to find out how much potential they had. To try harder to coax her into giving him a chance to help her overcome whatever was holding her back.

And perhaps, before today was over, he'd find an opportunity to begin laying that groundwork by showing her just how much he cared for her.

* * *

"Becca! Sam! Wait up!"

Rebecca turned at the familiar voice, smiling as Laura and Nick walked toward them hand in hand.

"Don't worry. You have a captive audience. Brad's still gabbing." Sam's lips quirked as she bounced Emily on her shoulder. "That's one of the downsides of being the preacher's wife. You're always the last to leave church."

"Are you complaining?" Laura's mouth twitched.

"Not a chance. He's worth waiting for any day."

"I know what you mean." Laura looked up at Nick, her features softening as they exchanged a tender glance. Then she extended her hand. "It's good to see you, Becca. And this must be Isabel and Zach. Sam told me you'd invited them to join you for Easter."

"That's right." Rebecca introduced them.

Laura studied Zach, faint furrows denting her brow. "Have we met before? You look familiar."

"Not formally. But you two were having dinner at Rebecca's restaurant a few weeks ago when I was there. I noticed you when Rebecca brought your dessert out."

"That's right." Laura's forehead smoothed out. "After she talked to us, Rebecca joined you at your table."

"You two ate together?" Sam raised her eyebrows.

"No." Rebecca tightened her grip on her purse. Her family was way too quick to jump to conclusions. "We just had coffee."

"But dinner would have been better." Zach grinned at Sam. "However, coffee was all I could manage to waylay her for that night. Fortunately, I see her regularly now thanks to this little lady." He laid a hand on Isabel's shoulder.

"I'm glad to hear that." Her father gave a pleased nod. "Rebecca could use some male companionship."

"Dad!" Heat flooded her cheeks.

"What's he done now?" Brad came up behind her, took one look at her flaming face, and slipped an arm around her shoulders. "Never mind. I can guess." He turned to Zach and introduced himself, keeping his arm around her.

Sweet of him to shift into protective mode.

"Rebecca speaks of you often. I'm glad we have the chance to meet." Zach returned his handshake, his gaze flicking to Brad's arm. Smart man that he was, he no doubt got Brad's treat-my-sister-with-care-or-you'll-answer-to-me message.

"So am I. I try to keep up with the events—and people—in her life. She's very special to me."

"She's very special to me too."

Zach's gaze didn't waver as he looked at her brother—and based on Brad's expression, the man she'd brought to dinner had passed muster.

"We're going to take off. " Laura linked her fingers with Nick's. "Happy Easter, everyone."

As the two of them left, Brad removed his arm from her shoulders and dropped onto the balls of his feet beside Isabel, who was clinging to her hand. "You must be Isabel." He smiled at her. "I'm Rebecca's brother. We're glad you came to visit us. What do you think of my new little girl?"

"She's pretty."

"Yes, she is. Would you like to hold her later?"

"Could I?" Her eyes widened.

"I think we can make that happen."

"We should head home." Sam shifted Emily in her arms. "The newest member of the clan is getting hungry."

Brad stood. "I'm ready. We'll meet you all there." He took Emily from Sam, and the two of them strolled toward the side of the church where Brad always parked.

Zach turned to her. "Ready?"

"Yes." Keeping a firm grip on Isabel's hand, Rebecca fell in beside him as they walked to the parking lot.

"You have a nice family." Zach pulled out his keys.

"I do. And I love them all dearly. But they can be a little too outspoken at times. Except Brad, of course. He's very diplomatic."

"And very protective."

So he *had* tuned in to her brother's subliminal message.

"We've always been close. He's been my champion as far back as I can remember."

"Everybody should have one of those." He opened the back door of the car and settled Isabel into the booster seat, then took his place behind the wheel. "You want to be my navigator again?"

"Sure. It's not far."

She guided him the short distance, and ten minutes later they pulled up in front of the house.

"Nice." Zach gave the mid-century modern a once-over as he set the brake.

"It suits them. But I'm more drawn to the traditional Cape Cod style. And one of these days, I'll trade in my apartment for one." She opened her door. "I hope everyone's hungry. Sam's upped her cooking game since she married Brad, so I expect we're in for a treat."

And they were. Her sister-in-law had outdone herself on their Easter meal.

Once they all ate their fill, Rebecca leaned back and smiled at her. "That was wonderful, Sam."

"I hope you saved room for dessert."

"I'm not sure I can eat another bite."

"I can." Zach grinned. "I never pass up a sweet treat."

"Coming right up. Brad, you want to give me a hand?"

"Sure."

The two of them disappeared into the kitchen while Henry entertained the rest of them with a story about a woman from their hometown whose chickens kept escaping from her ever-expanding coop and invading her neighbors' yards. According to Henry, she'd been dubbed the fowl woman by said neighbors—and not in a flattering sense.

They were still chuckling over his animated narration when the kitchen door opened and Sam and Brad appeared, Sam holding a decorated cake topped with flickering candles while they both beamed at her. Then they launched into a hearty rendition of "Happy Birthday," with Henry joining in from the table.

What on earth?

When they finished, Isabel turned to her, brow puckered. "Is this your birthday?"

"No, sweetie. My birthday was a month ago." She scanned the three grinning faces. Zach seemed clueless, so he wasn't in on the unexpected party. "What's this all about?"

"You didn't think we'd let your birthday pass with nothing more than a phone call on the big day, did you?" Sam set the cake on the table in front of her. "We know it's late, but you can blame that on the little gal sleeping down the hall."

Rebecca shook her head. "You guys are too much. I didn't need a cake or a party."

"Yes, you did." Sam straightened up. "The fun factor in your life could use a boost. You should work on that with her, Zach."

"I try, but she's a hard sell."

"Be tenacious." Henry pointed a finger at him. "Persistence pays."

"Hey. No hassling the birthday girl." Brad's good-natured admonition put a stop to the discussion about her social life. "Go ahead, Rebecca. Make a wish and blow out the candles."

She closed her eyes.

But the wish was a no-brainer, now that Zach was in her life—even if it was a tall order.

She opened her eyes and extinguished the candles with one mighty breath.

"Well done." Sam grinned and set about cutting the cake. "You must have as much hot air as I do."

That drew a laugh, and as they all enjoyed their cake the conversation continued with more teasing and banter.

When the last bite was consumed, Sam leaned back and groaned. "I'll never lose the rest of the weight I put on with Emily if I keep this up."

"You look the same to me as you did before." Rebecca raised her coffee cup in salute.

"Thanks. But I've still got five pounds to go."

"Speaking of new babies…have you ever seen a real baby bunny up close, Isabel?" Henry angled toward her.

"No."

"Would you like to?"

"Do you have one?"

"No. But I know where there's a nest, and if we're real careful, I don't think the mama rabbit will mind if we take a quick look."

"Can I, Uncle Zach?"

"Sure. Just stay close to Rebecca's papa."

Her dad stood. "I'll keep a close eye on her." He held out his hand, and Isabel took it.

As the two of them disappeared toward the back of the house, Sam rose too. "Why don't you two stroll over to the park across the street while Brad and I clean up?"

Rebecca shook her head and pushed back from the table. "We can't leave you to deal with all these dishes. I'll help."

"Not today." Brad sent her the don't-mess-with-your-big-brother look he used to use whenever he dug in his heels while they were growing up. "You deal with kitchen duties every day. We can manage here. You and Zach take a walk."

"I hate leaving other people with all the work."

Sam rolled her eyes. "Listen to your brother. You're our guest today. Plus, it's a belated birthday celebration. So you are *not* going to do dishes. Period. End of discussion. That's final."

She arched an eyebrow at Brad, eyes twinkling. "Should I be a little more forceful, do you think?"

His mouth flexed. "I think you made your point. Go ahead, you two. We'll be here when you get back. And Henry will keep Isabel entertained."

Rebecca sent Zach an uncertain look.

If she wanted this relationship to progress, now was as good a time as any to test the waters. Besides, things couldn't get too touchy-feely in a public park in broad daylight. Settings didn't get much safer than that. And she ought to be able to handle a simple kiss, if Zach was inclined to steal one.

Which he very well might be, based on the slow simmer in his irises.

Nevertheless, he left the decision up to her.

She took a steadying breath. "If Zach's willing, a circuit of the park would be lovely."

"I'm in." Zero hesitation on his part.

"We won't be gone long." She stood.

"Don't hurry on our account." Sam began gathering up the plates as Zach rose.

Rebecca led the way to the door, Zach in her wake, but when they stepped outside he fell in beside her and reached for her hand. Entwined his fingers with hers and lifted their linked hands. "This okay?"

Her heart warmed.

Zach didn't seem like the type who would ask permission to initiate such a simple gesture. He was more the type who trusted his instincts and his ability to read signals from a woman, and knew when the sparks zipping around in the air weren't one-way.

But kudos to him for also realizing—and respecting—that a woman who'd been clear about her unwillingness to date might not appreciate even an innocent display of affection.

Her nerves quieted.

If he was that sensitive in such a small matter, he wasn't likely to push her beyond her comfort level. Especially in a public park.

"Yes."

She was rewarded with a smile and a gentle squeeze of her fingers.

Yet as they crossed the street and began their slow circuit of the park under the canopy of flowering trees, the tingle in her nerve endings intensified.

The setting was conducive to romance, and she had no doubt her companion had romance on his mind. At the very least, a kiss or two could be in the offing.

A prospect that jacked up her pulse with sweet anticipation—but also trepidation.

For if that came to pass, there was no way to predict what would happen despite her comfort level at the moment.

9

She was as nervous as the whistleblowers in one of the high-stakes stories he covered, who had much to lose if they were identified as his confidential source.

But Rebecca had nothing to fear from him.

Zach slanted her a glance as they strolled through the quiet park and gave her fingers another reassuring squeeze.

Didn't help.

Nervous energy continued to ping from her.

Unless she relaxed, this walk was going to be a total bust.

Diversion tactics were in order.

"I had a note from Josef this morning."

Her forehead rumpled. "How is everything?"

"No better. Maybe worse, in fact. He's not a complainer, so it's hard to tell. But it's obvious the situation over there continues to be dicey, and he misses Isabel desperately."

"I'm not surprised. The bond between the two of them is easy to see." Rebecca exhaled. "I know she's anxious to go home, but I'm dreading the day we have to send her back to that environment."

"Me too. On a happier note, my problem student is turning things around."

"Pete Cramer?"

"Yes. I heard some teachers in the lounge talking the other

day, speculating on why he's suddenly buckled down and gotten serious about his studies."

Her mouth bowed. "I could clear up that mystery in one word—you."

"I may have been the catalyst, but you were the inspiration. His turnaround started after I followed your advice and offered encouragement and discipline. He's also been talking about applying for that week-long writing camp this summer in Michigan I told you about. The biggest hurdle is funding."

"Do they offer scholarships?"

"Yes, but his academic record to date doesn't warrant one, even if I write a letter of recommendation. He's starting to look for a part-time job to earn enough to secure a spot if he's accepted."

Rebecca sidestepped an earlier egg-hunt casualty, the painted shell cracked and the hard-boiled stuffing smashed. "Do you think he'd be a reliable worker?"

"Yes."

"One of my part-time high school servers is quitting next week. Her family is moving. I'd be happy to interview Pete."

His throat tightened.

Was there no end to this woman's generosity?

"That would be fantastic. Thank you."

"I'm always happy to help people who need a leg up. Tell me a bit more about him."

He complied while they continued their walk, but as they neared the end of their circuit, he motioned to a bench up ahead. "Would you like to sit for a few minutes?"

She hesitated as she focused on a bed of colorful tulips in the center of the park, the flowers waving in the gentle breeze. Moistened her lips. "Yes."

While they walked over to it, Zach released the breath he'd been holding.

When they sat, he kept a discreet distance between them. But he rested his arm on the back of the bench, behind her. Close, yet not touching.

Yet.

He angled toward her. "I had a good time today."

Her answering smile seemed a tad shaky. "Me too."

"Your family was sweet to give us some time together."

She shifted. Linked her fingers in her lap. "Except they have a tendency to jump to conclusions."

"They didn't have to jump far with me. I've been champing at the bit for time alone with you for weeks—as you know. I'm hoping your willingness to take a walk with me today may mean you've softened your no-dating stance. Does it?" Watching her face for any hint of a back-off signal, he lifted his hand and fingered a lock of her soft hair.

Her breath hitched. "A little."

Music to his ears.

He eased closer on the bench and let his other hand migrate to her shoulder, stroking his fingers gently back and forth. Then, his gaze riveted on hers, he leaned slowly toward her, still scrutinizing her for any sign she objected to him getting up close and personal.

All he saw in her eyes was a longing so intense it stole the breath from his lungs.

That was a green light in his playbook.

He closed the remaining distance between them and lowered his mouth to hers in a simple kiss, gentle and uncomplicated, as light as a drifting leaf. It was a testing…a tasting…a trying on for size.

And her innocent sweetness—her artless response akin to that of an inexperienced schoolgirl—sent a shock wave through him despite her warning that she didn't date.

She was nothing like the practiced women of his acquaintance, who were well-versed in flirtation and romance.

And he wanted more.

Because kissing Rebecca was like his first taste of cotton candy as a kid. Heady, intoxicating, and infinitely sweet as it dissolved on his tongue.

But just as he prepared to deepen the kiss a bit, approaching voices intruded.

It sounded like a family group, also out for a stroll.

Blast.

He couldn't care less if he was caught in a clinch, but Rebecca would be embarrassed.

Reluctantly he eased back.

She leaned after him, prolonging the kiss, clearly unaware of the approaching audience.

Summoning up every ounce of his willpower, he drew farther back, just enough to break contact. "There's someone coming." He spoke softly as the warmth of her choppy breath caressed his face.

For a moment she remained a whisper away. Then she straightened up, eyes dazed.

He kept his focus on her while the family passed, the children chattering as they headed in the direction of the playground he and Rebecca had passed during their walk.

"I, uh, guess we should go b-back." Her voice was as uneven as her respiration.

There was no going back to their previous platonic relationship, but yeah, they should return to the house. Even if that was the last thing he wanted to do.

Because now that he'd tasted her lips, he wanted—needed—more.

The good news?

Based on her response just now, there would be more opportunities to do exactly that.

The sooner the better.

* * *

Zach had kissed her, and she hadn't panicked.

That in itself was an Easter miracle.

As she peeked over at him while he drove the three of them back to Ste. Genevieve, her lips curved up.

As if sensing her perusal, he looked over. Warmth filled his eyes before he refocused on the road. "I had fun today."

"Me too."

"Especially during our walk." He flicked her another quick glance.

"Me too."

"I had fun seeing the baby rabbits." Isabel joined in from the back seat. "Your papa is nice, Becca."

She angled around. "Yes, he is."

"My papa is nice too." She looked down and fiddled with the ruffle on her dress. "I missed him a lot today."

Pressure built in Rebecca's throat, and she reached back to take Isabel's hand. "I know, sweetie."

"He won't be here for my birthday, either."

Which was coming up fast, as she and Zach had discussed.

"He'll be here in his heart. And Uncle Zach and I will help you celebrate. I'll make a special dinner for you. What would you like to have?"

She caught her lower lip between her teeth for a moment, then ticked off the items. “Spaghetti and French fries and corn on the cob and chocolate cake.”

“That’s not the most nutritious menu I’ve ever heard, but it *is* your birthday.” Rebecca smiled at her. “We’ll have exactly what you want. And maybe we could have a slumber party too.”

Isabel cocked her head. “What’s that?”

“It’s an all-night party. You’d bring your pajamas over and sleep at my apartment. We’d make cookies and watch movies and stay up late.”

“Could Uncle Zach come too?”

Whoops.

“Could I?” He waggled his eyebrows at her, eyes twinkling.

He was no help.

“There’s room in the bed.” Isabel was growing more interested by the minute. “Rebecca has a big bed.”

Oh brother.

“Slumber parties are, uh, just for girls.” Rebecca tried to tame the heat creeping across her cheeks.

“Oh.” Isabel’s face fell. “I wish Uncle Zach could come.”

“So does Uncle Zach.” He grinned toward the passenger seat. “But Rebecca’s right, honey. The kind of slumber party *she’s* talking about is just for girls.”

“But we’ll still have lots of fun.” Rebecca ignored Zach’s smirk.

“Okay then, I guess.”

They chatted a bit more about birthday plans, but as they drew close to Ste. Genevieve Isabel’s eyelids grew heavy and she dozed off.

“Is she out?” Zach checked on her in the rearview mirror when silence descended in the car.

"Like a light. Too much sugar."

They finished the short remaining drive to her apartment in companionable silence, and when Zach pulled up in front he spoke as he set the brake. "I'll walk you to your door."

"You don't have to do that. Stay with Isabel."

He angled toward the back seat and gave her a scan. "She'll never miss me, and I can see the car from your door."

Without giving her a chance to argue, he slid from behind the wheel, softly closed the door, and circled the car.

She got out and was waiting, key in hand, when he reached the passenger side.

"You're not letting me be a gentleman." He motioned toward her car door.

"Sorry. I'm used to taking care of myself. But if it's any consolation, I appreciate that you *look* like a gentleman. If I didn't tell you earlier, that's a beautiful suit." And it was. The charcoal-gray jacket emphasized his broad shoulders and lean physique, and his crisp white shirt, paired with a burgundy-and-silver tie, could have come from a GQ ad. He was impressive, distinguished, suave, and incredibly handsome.

But she confined her compliments to his suit.

"Thanks. I don't wear one often. Shall we?" He motioned toward her door, then wove his fingers through hers.

A delicious tingle shivered down her spine.

Maybe he had another kiss in mind.

And since the last one had gone so well, she had no objections.

The subtle but heady scent of his aftershave swirled around her as they walked to her apartment and ascended the two steps that led to her small front porch, an intoxicating aroma that disrupted the rhythm of her breathing.

At the door, she inserted her key, twisted it until the lock clicked, then dropped it back into her purse.

Only then did she risk a peek at Zach.

He'd propped a shoulder against the porch post, arms folded, and when their gazes connected he hitched up one side of his mouth. "Home safe and sound." His casual stance and relaxed tone were at odds with the intensity in his eyes.

"Yes." It was all she could manage.

"We got interrupted at the park."

She swallowed. "I know."

After a moment he pushed off from the post and crossed to her, irises darkening. "We should finish what we started."

This was her chance to back off. Say no.

But she didn't.

Because she wasn't afraid.

"Maybe we should." Her agreement came out in a whisper.

That was all the invitation he needed.

He erased the remaining distance between them. Lifted one hand and slipped it around to her nape, his thumb playing gently with the lobe of her ear. Then he moved her hair aside, lowered his head, and nuzzled her neck.

Oh, mercy.

Was this the Fourth of July?

Because fireworks were going off somewhere.

She arched forward to meet his kiss as his lips lingered in the hollow of throat. Sighed when they moved across her cheek, up to her forehead. Her eyelids drifted closed—and when he kissed each one tenderly a sweet shiver rippled through her.

This was like no kiss she'd ever had.

And when he cupped her face with his hands and claimed her lips, she slipped her arms around his neck.

The sound of his sharply indrawn breath registered when she tunneled her fingers through the soft hair at the base of his head, but the magic of his kiss short-circuited the left side of her brain.

Until the mood of the embrace shifted from pleasurable exploration to passionate and he pressed against her, pinning her spine to the wall, his hands trapping her on either side as he let his lips do the caressing.

All at once the familiar suffocating panic, the feeling of helplessness and entrapment, came roaring back.

Her lungs shut down, and despite her desperate attempt to pull in air, they refused to cooperate as his weight immobilized her. As his lips moved from seeking to demanding. As his arms became steel cables imprisoning her.

Mustering every ounce of her strength, she tried to push him back.

But she had no leverage from her hemmed-in position.

Uttering a barely there whimper, she at last managed to wrench her lips free and turn her head a bit as she gasped for air. "Stop."

It was more wheeze than word, but it was enough to get Zach's attention.

He backed up a few inches. Despite the dim evening light, it was easy to read the confusion in his eyes. "What's wrong?"

"I need to g-go in." He was still too close for her to turn, so she fumbled behind her for the knob.

"Why? What's going on?"

"Just let me go. Please." She tried to twist around.

He didn't budge. "Not until you tell me what's wrong."

Her panic ratcheted up again and she pushed against his chest. "Let me go. Please."

His eyes narrowed as he scrutinized her, and then he dropped his arms. Stepped back.

She sucked in air as he gave her space.

"I don't understand what's happening." There was no anger in his voice. Just bewilderment. "I thought you wanted me to kiss you."

"I-I did. This isn't y-your fault."

He studied her in the dim light as silent seconds ticked by, and when he spoke, his voice was soft. "I scared you, didn't I?"

May as well admit the truth. Denying the obvious would be foolish. "Y-yes."

He ran his fingers through his hair. Blew out a breath. "I'm sorry. I guess I got carried away. I never intended to frighten you. Just the opposite."

The rational side of her brain knew that. But she also knew now that she wasn't equipped to deal with a man of strong passions like Zach. Hard as she'd tried to open her heart to him, to subdue the terror, she'd failed miserably, just as she'd feared.

"I know." A silent tear rolled down her cheek, and she reached up to brush it away with shaking fingers. "It would be better if you don't waste any more of your time on me."

"I don't consider the time I spend with you wasted. I care about you." Twin crevices dented his brow "I don't want things to end like this, Rebecca. Please tell me what's going on."

"You w-wouldn't understand."

"Would you at least give me a chance to try?"

Despite his gentle entreaty, she shook her head.

Because what was there to say? She'd hoped—prayed—that this time would be different. But it wasn't.

And it never would be, if a kind and principled man like Zach couldn't banish her fear.

"Look…we need to talk about this." There was a hint of desperation in his voice now. "Not tonight, I know, but how about tomorrow, in the daylight, somewhere you feel safe? Just name the place and time."

Rebecca's vision misted.

He was trying so hard. Showing more patience than she had a right to expect after the ego dent she'd just given him. But seeing him in any capacity that didn't involve caring for Isabel would only be hurtful and delay the inevitable.

"Thank you for offering, but it's no use." She fumbled behind her for the door handle again. "You need someone who can love you like you deserve to be loved." She twisted the knob, slipped through, and closed the door. Clicked the lock into place.

Five seconds later, a knock sounded. "Rebecca, please don't shut me out." His distraught voice came through the door.

She backed away.

And though he tried again, she ignored him even as her stomach coiled into a hard knot.

Because walking away was best for him, even if it broke *her* heart.

* * *

Zach stared at Rebecca's closed door, gut twisting.

How could he walk away, leaving things like this between them?

But he couldn't make her talk to him, and the little girl waiting for him in the back seat needed his attention.

Expelling a hard breath, he turned and walked back to his car.

It didn't take a genius to realize Rebecca had been frightened just now. No, scratch that. She'd been in full panic mode. All from a simple kiss she'd consented to.

It didn't make sense.

That's why they needed to talk ASAP. Because there was no way he could mitigate her fear if he didn't know its source.

As he circled around to the driver's side and slid behind the wheel, he glanced back at Isabel. She was still sound asleep, her jaw slack, utter peace on her face.

But there'd been no peace in Rebecca's taut features, and her eyes had been filled with misery, loneliness, and utter despair. Tension had radiated from every pore in her body, and she'd been poised for flight, ready to bolt at the slightest provocation after he'd backed off.

He put the car in gear and pointed it toward his apartment.

Maybe he'd gotten a little carried away and come on a bit too strong after tasting her tantalizing sweetness, but not enough to induce her frenzied response.

There were larger issues at work here. Ones he needed to uncover if he ever hoped to make inroads on her heart.

His number one priority.

Because he couldn't let this kind, caring, intelligent, loyal woman slip out of his life without a fight. Not that he'd ever force his attentions on someone who was uninterested, but Rebecca was interested. He'd bet his life on that.

Now he just had to convince her to trust him.

A monumental task based on what had just happened.

At that depressing thought, a shroud of gloom settled over him.

How could a day that had started off so upbeat end like this?

His phone pinged with a text as he pulled into his parking spot, and once he set the brake he pulled out his cell.

It was from Rebecca.

Pulse picking up, he clicked on the icon to read the entire message.

> I'm sorry for the meltdown. The blame is all mine. And it will happen again with another kiss. Please accept that and write me off. However, I'll continue to honor my commitment to helping with Isabel. In return I ask that you honor my request to follow a hands-off rule going forward. For the record, I did enjoy spending Easter with you.

He hesitated.

Hands-off would be tough.

But if he didn't agree to follow her ground rule, she'd back off. And that wouldn't be fair to Isabel. If Rebecca disappeared from her world, it would only further disrupt her life.

And his.

Taking a deep breath, he attached a thumbs-up emoji to her message.

Then, Brad's sermon echoing in his mind, he sent a plea heavenward for the wisdom and guidance to give Rebecca the warmth and patient nurturing that would help her heart bloom again.

10

Why was Zach calling her at nine-thirty at night?

As her cell trilled, Rebecca stared at the screen.

In the week and a half since Easter, he'd respected her wishes to keep things cordial but hands-off, even though his eyes were always filled with questions—and desire.

A very unsettling combination.

That's why she'd made sure Isabel was always around when they interacted. He couldn't get into a personal discussion in the little girl's presence.

But maybe he'd tired of her evasion tactic and had decided a phone call was in order.

Not a discussion she wanted to have tonight. Or ever.

After three rings, the call rolled to voicemail.

Less than thirty seconds later, a new voicemail appeared in her inbox.

Taking a deep breath, she played it back.

"Sorry to bother you at this hour, Rebecca. But I have a problem with Isabel. Please call ASAP."

Uh-oh.

Pulse accelerating at his taut voice, she dialed him at once.

He picked up on the first ring, his voice as tense as it had been in the voicemail. "I know it's late, but can you come over?"

"What's wrong?"

"Isabel was drifting off to sleep when a couple of kids set off fireworks right outside her window. Given her circumstances at home, I'm guessing she thought it was gunfire. She freaked out, and I can't get through to her. I'm hoping you might be able to."

"I'm on my way."

Rebecca ended the call, snatched up her purse, and dashed for her car. Her experience with traumatized children was negligible, but she'd do what she could.

As she hurried toward Zach's door less than ten minutes later, he pulled it open. She slipped past him into the eerily quiet apartment, turning as he set the lock. "Where is she?"

"In the bedroom. I heard her cry out when the fireworks started, and by the time I got to her she was huddled on the floor with her doll, shaking. I tried talking to her, but it's like she can't hear me. She looks like she's crying, but there's almost no sound. And there aren't any tears." He drew a ragged breath and wiped a hand down his face. "I'm sorry to bother you, but I didn't know what else to do."

"It's okay." She set her purse on a nearby chair. "I'm no expert at this either, though."

Heart pounding, she crossed to the bedroom and paused on the threshold.

The scene fit Zach's description. Isabel was huddled against the wall, knees pulled up, face pale, eyes glassy. Her frail shoulders were shaking, and she clutched Raggedy Ann against her chest.

Rebecca took a fortifying breath, entered the room, and dropped to her knees beside the traumatized child. "It's okay, sweetie. You're safe." She brushed some stray strands of hair back from the wan face. A shudder ran through Isabel, but she continued to stare straight ahead. "Would you like me to hold you?"

No response.

It was almost as if she was in shock.

A tingle of fear snaked down Rebecca's spine.

She was way out of her depth here.

A quick glance at Zach's panicked face told her he felt the same.

But someone had to do *something*.

She forced up the corners of her stiff lips. "Well, I'm going to sit here next to you." She positioned herself on one side of the little girl. "Uncle Zach will sit with us too." She motioned him over.

He crossed the room in a few long strides and dropped down to sit on Isabel's other side.

As she began stroking Isabel's arm, Rebecca looked over at him and mouthed the words "touch her." He did so at once, mirroring her actions. "Remember that song I sang to you the first night you were here, Isabel? Why don't I sing it again?" Without waiting for a reply, she launched into the familiar children's song. She sang all the verses she could recall, and as she neared the end there was a slight softening in Isabel's rigid posture.

Thank you, God!

When that song wound down, she started in on another. After she ran out of children's tunes, she resorted to songs from musicals and hymns.

Much to her surprise, Zach's rich baritone joined her on a few. He stumbled over some of the lyrics, but his valiant attempt warmed her heart.

She sang for almost twenty minutes, never breaking physical contact with Isabel, and bit by bit the little girl's muscles went limp, until finally her sobs became more pronounced and the tears began to flow.

When Isabel reached for her, Rebecca pulled her onto her lap and held her tight, stroking her back and rocking her gently. Over her head, Rebecca caught Zach's eye. "I think we'll be okay now."

At her quiet comment, relief chased the tension from his features and he rose. "I'll get her a glass of water."

As he disappeared out the door, Isabel spoke through her tears. "I want my m-mama and p-papa."

"I know, sweetie. I'm sorry they can't be here with you. But Uncle Zach and I love you very much. And we promised your papa we'd take care of you until you go home."

She snuggled closer. "S-sometimes it was s-scary at home, when the guns went off." Her voice was so soft Rebecca had to lean close to hear it. "Mr. Kramar on the f-first floor got shot once. I saw it happen from our window. A-after that my papa would make me get d-down on the floor whenever there was trouble. He told me there wouldn't be any shooting here, but t-tonight I thought I heard guns."

Rebecca blinked to clear her vision. This child had been through far too much at her tender age. "It was just fireworks, sweetie, like Uncle Zach told you. You don't have to be scared. We promised your papa that we'd keep you safe, and we will."

Zach reentered with the glass of water and dropped down beside them again.

"Would you like a drink, Isabel? Uncle Zach brought you some water."

When the girl turned to look at him, Zach touched her cheek. "Rebecca's right, Isabel. We won't let anything hurt you."

She took the glass, gulped some water, and handed the tumbler back to him. "I wish my papa was here."

"I do too, honey. He misses you as much as you miss him.

But just think of all the stories you'll have to tell him about America when you go home."

She considered that for a moment. "Like he used to tell *me* stories about America."

"That's right."

When she yawned, Rebecca smoothed back her hair and looked at Zach. "I think it's way past someone's bedtime."

Taking her cue, he reached for Isabel, then extended a hand to her.

"Will you stay with me for a little while, Becca? Please?" Isabel held out her hand as Zach tucked her into bed.

Rebecca moved closer and folded the small fingers in hers. "I'll do better than that. I'll lie beside you until you go to sleep. How does that sound?"

The ghost of a smile flickered at the corners of her mouth. "Good."

"Is that all right with you?" Rebecca glanced at Zach. She probably should have asked first, but after all that had happened tonight, her brain wasn't firing on all cylinders.

"Of course. I have some papers to read, anyway." He kissed Isabel goodnight and walked toward the door, shutting it halfway as he exited.

Rebecca stretched out beside Isabel, and the girl scooted over to cuddle against her. With all the emotional turmoil of the evening, she'd no doubt be asleep in minutes.

Until then, though, why not relax and relish this sweet taste of mothering her heart had always craved?

* * *

Zach pushed the last paper aside and glanced at his watch. Blinked.

How could it be eleven already?

And why was Rebecca still here?

He stood and made his way to Isabel's door, pausing on the threshold to peek inside.

Rebecca lay on her side, one arm over Isabel, her hair splayed on the pillow behind her. Isabel's back was cuddled against Rebecca, her Raggedy Ann still tucked close at hand.

His throat pinched.

In sleep, the two of them were the picture of vulnerable innocence. And they activated a latent protective instinct that was so strong his lungs locked for a moment.

What a strange feeling for a guy who'd never wanted to be responsible for anything except the accuracy and credibility of his reporting.

But there it was, like it or not.

And truth be told, he liked it.

A lot.

Having these two special people in his life these past weeks had given him a tantalizing and appealing taste of family life, albeit a temporary one.

But more and more he was hoping Rebecca might play a permanent role in his life.

If she ever gave him an opening to address whatever fears were holding her back.

She stirred…then hesitated, as if orienting herself. After a moment she checked on Isabel and rose, picking up her shoes before padding to the door.

Only as she approached did she notice him standing there.

"I was just coming to check on both of you." He spoke first, lest she think he'd been playing peeping Tom.

"Sorry. I fell asleep. What time is it?" When he told her, her eyes widened. "Wow. I need to go home." She continued to the living room and sat to put her shoes back on. "You may be off on Saturday, but that's my busiest day."

"I'm sorry I disturbed your sleep tonight."

"No worries. To be honest, I'm surprised something like this hasn't happened before, with all that Isabel's been through."

"Me too. I'm hoping it's a one-off. How's Pete doing at the restaurant?" The non sequitur earned him a surprised glance, but at this hour a natural segue had eluded him. And he wanted to talk to her. Their conversations lately were so abbreviated during Isabel's handoffs before and after school that no more than housekeeping matters were discussed.

"Fine. He's a hard worker."

"I'm glad to hear that. I had some other good news today too. My editor called. They're going to run my series on government corruption. One of my sources came forward on his own, with plenty of documentation to validate my story."

She sent him a quick smile as she tied her other shoe. "I'm sure that made your day."

"From a vindication standpoint, yes. But I was going over a paper with Pete when the call came in, and to be honest it felt more like an unwanted distraction. In some ways, my investigative work seems like a lifetime ago."

"But you still plan to go back to your job when your leave is up, don't you?"

"I haven't thought much about it, between learning the ropes at school and caring for Isabel." He flicked a glance toward the bedroom. Sighed. "I hate the thought of sending her back to that turmoil, even though I know Josef will do his best to protect her."

"Has he given you any idea when he'd like her to come back?"

"Yeah." He dropped into the chair across from her. "That's my other piece of news for the day. He emailed this morning. He's looking at three weeks from now."

Rebecca's forehead bunched. "Has the situation improved over there?"

"No. But he doesn't want to impose any longer. I'm not sure what to tell him. The timing of my leave was almost providential, but trying to take care of her back in the city with the crazy hours I work would be a challenge. Plus, she'd have to make another huge adjustment. Sending her home would be less traumatic in many ways."

"But more dangerous."

"Yeah." He couldn't argue with that.

"I guess we'll just have to ask God to watch over her." She stood, and the distress in her eyes mirrored the angst in his heart. "But saying goodbye to her will be wrenching."

"I know." He walked with her to the door and watched until she was safely in her car.

Yet as she drove away, his greatest fear was that bidding farewell to Isabel wouldn't be the only goodbye he'd have to say in the very near future.

For once his little guest was gone, he'd have no more excuse to see the woman who was fast winning his heart.

* * *

"Which present would you like to open first?" Rebecca arranged the wrapped packages on her coffee table and smiled at Isabel. "Or are you too full after the spaghetti, French fries, corn, and chocolate cake?"

"I'm not too full." She gave the gifts an eager scan.

"Why don't you start with Uncle Zach's?" Rebecca handed it over and sat across from the duo on her couch.

Isabel tore off the colorful paper, eyes sparkling when a child-sized backpack decorated with characters from a popular animated children's movie emerged. "It's beautiful! Thank you, Uncle Zach. I can use it when I start school this year." She reached up and gave him a hug around the neck.

Rebecca handed her the next gift, two boxes tied together with ribbon. "These are from me. The first one is for when you start writing."

As with Zach's gift, Isabel made short work of the paper.

From the first box, she pulled out a ballpoint pen with her name engraved on it. The second held a pink sweater with a heart applique on the pocket.

"I love these, Becca! Thank you." She trotted over to dispense another hug.

"The last one is your papa's present, honey." Zach picked it up and settled it in her lap when she returned to the couch.

She cradled it in her hands for a moment, then carefully tore off the paper to reveal a carved wooden box. "Ooh. I bet my papa made this." She ran her fingers over the intricate handiwork. "He's a good carver." She lifted the lid. Inside, on a red velvet lining, rested a folded sheet of paper and another, smaller package.

Isabel removed the package first and unwrapped it, fishing through the tissue to extract a delicate filigreed gold brooch. The front was hinged, and she flipped it open to reveal a photograph of a couple. No doubt Josef and Katrina. "This was my mama's." Her voice was hushed. "She always told me someday it would be mine."

Pressure built in Rebecca's throat, and when she met Zach's

gaze there was a suspicious sheen in his eyes too.

Isabel withdrew the single sheet of paper in the case and unfolded it, frowning at the words before looking up at Zach. "Would you read it to me?"

Zach smoothed back her hair. "Of course, honey." He took it and spoke the words Josef had penned.

"'My dearest Isabel, I am so sorry I cannot be with you to celebrate your seventh birthday. But I will be thinking of you all day, and hoping you have fun with Uncle Zach and Rebecca. Wasn't it nice of them to have a party for you?

'I made you this treasure box, which you can fill with special things that are important to you. I have given you the first treasure to put in it, the brooch your mama loved so much. Remember how she always wore it near her heart? I hope you will do the same, my child, to remind you that your mama and I will always be close to you, even when we are far away.

'I miss you, little one, more than words can say. You are my sunlight and my joy. Your mama always used to say that God gave us a touch of heaven when he sent you to us, and I believe she was right. You are a precious gift, and I love you with all my heart. I am counting the days until you are home with me again.

'Happy birthday, Isabel. And may God be with you.'"

As the last few words scratched past Zach's throat, a tear slipped from Rebecca's eye. But she wiped it away and took a steadying breath. They needed to cheer Isabel up, not depress her.

"You're a very lucky girl to have such a wonderful father." She managed to coax up the corners of her lips.

"I know." She fingered the delicate brooch and stared at the photograph of the smiling man and woman. "I miss him. And I miss my mama. She was pretty, wasn't she?"

"Yes, she was. Would you like me to pin the brooch on for you?"

Isabel nodded, and Rebecca knelt in front of her to secure it to her sweater.

"They're right by my heart now, aren't they?" Isabel touched the brooch.

"Yes, they are."

"Can we call Papa now?" She angled toward Zach.

Rebecca sent him a quick look.

This was where it was going to get even harder—because Zach had already alerted her that Josef wasn't in a position tonight to schedule a call.

Zach put his arm around Isabel, and Rebecca tucked herself in on the other side of the little girl. "I got an email from him a couple of hours ago, honey. He's working in a place tonight where he can't talk on the phone. But he promised to do his best to call you tomorrow."

At her crestfallen expression, Rebecca's heart ached. "You know he'd talk to you if he could, don't you, sweetie?" She took her hand.

"Yes." Her forehead puckered and she looked back at Zach. "He's not sick like Mama was, is he?"

"No. He's fine. But the kind of work he does makes it hard for him to talk on the phone sometimes."

"I know." She heaved a sigh. "He used to tell that to Mama. But she always said it was important work and I should be happy I had such a good man for a father. And she said we should be brave." She dipped her chin and stroked a hand over the carvings on the box Josef had made. "I try, but it's hard being brave."

"Yes, it is." Zach's Adam's apple bobbed as he touched her hair.

A tear leaked from the corner of Rebecca's eye, and she stood. She had to get away before she lost it. "Zach, let me refill your coffee." She picked up his nearly full cup and fled to the kitchen before he could respond.

Maybe leaving him alone to comfort Isabel was the coward's way out, but she'd be no use if the floodgates opened.

She leaned against the refrigerator and closed her eyes. Took slow, deep breaths.

But the knot in her stomach didn't loosen.

How could they send that poor child back to the danger and turmoil in her country?

Yet what choice did they have?

It was clear Josef loved her more than anything on earth. The treasure box he'd crafted was only the latest evidence of his devotion. How many lonely nights had he spent since her departure carving it with painstaking care in his silent and empty apartment?

Isabel needed to be with the father she loved and who loved her in return.

But would he be able to protect her when she went home?

11

At the sound of shattering dishes for the second time in an hour, Rebecca frowned and glanced up from the computer in her tiny office at the restaurant.

What was going on out there?

Whatever was happening, it was distracting her from the paperwork she'd hoped to get done while two of her high school servers set up for tomorrow's special luncheon.

But from the sound of it, her profits from that event were going down the drain.

As she pushed back from her desk to investigate, a tentative knock sounded on her half-closed door and Pete Cramer stuck his head in. "I'm sorry to bother you, Ms. Matthews, but I think there's something wrong with Melanie." His forehead wrinkled. "She looks kind of funny. I asked her if she was sick, but she said no."

"Are you two about finished?"

"We'll be done in ten minutes."

"Tell Melanie I'd like to see her after you're finished. You can lock the door behind you as you leave."

"Okay. Thanks. But please don't say I said anything. She might not appreciate me butting in."

"I won't."

Rebecca swiveled back to her computer and continued to

work until another knock sounded on her door.

"Come in." She called the invitation over her shoulder as she finished updating a spreadsheet. "I'll be with you in a minute."

When she turned toward the teen less than thirty seconds later, Melanie was still hovering on the threshold, complexion pale, features strained. She looked nothing like her usual cheerful, smiling self.

No wonder Pete had raised a red flag.

"I'm really sorry about the dishes, Ms. Matthews." There was a trace of tears in Melanie's voice. "You can take the cost out of my pay."

"Don't worry about it, Melanie." Rebecca put as much empathy and reassurance in her tone as she could. "I'm more concerned about you. You've been working for me for nine months, and I don't think you've ever dropped a plate or glass, let alone a tray. Is everything all right?"

"Yes." Melanie wiped the palms of her hands down her jeans and focused on the floor. "I…I guess so."

At the shaky caveat, Rebecca stood and circled the desk. Touched the girl's arm. "Would you like to have a soda and talk for a few minutes? I'm not a bad listener."

She caught her lower lip between her teeth. Wrapped her arms around herself. Finally gave a jerky nod. "Okay."

"Go on into the restaurant. I'll get the sodas."

When Rebecca entered the dining room a couple of minutes later, Melanie was tucked into a corner table, shoulders hunched, misery etched on her face.

The teen took the soda in silence, but she didn't drink it or speak.

Some diplomatic probing was in order.

"Have you had some bad news, Melanie?" Perhaps her father

was being laid off. Rumor was the plant where he worked was downsizing. That would upset the whole family.

"No."

Rebecca took a sip of soda, her gaze falling on a bruise on Melanie's arm as the girl toyed with her straw. "What happened here?" She laid her fingers gently against the purple area.

Melanie flinched, and her pallor intensified.

Bingo.

The bruise was a clue to her present emotional distress.

"When did you do that?" Rebecca withdrew her hand and inclined her head to the bluish-black contusion.

"L-last night. I went to the end-of-school dance."

"I've had a few bruised toes from dancing, but never a bruised arm."

"It didn't happen at…at the dance. It happened later."

An alert began beeping in Rebecca's mind, but she kept her tone as neutral as she could. "Who did you go with?"

"J-Jack Simpson."

Since that was all she offered, the hard question would have to be asked.

"Did he do that to you, Melanie?" Rebecca used her gentlest voice despite the fury building inside her.

"Yes." Her voice was barely a whisper.

"What happened?"

"After the d-dance, he asked me if I wanted to drive to the lake. I thought he just wanted to, you know, make out a little, so I said yes. But it got really h-heavy."

Rebecca clenched her fingers in her lap. "How heavy?"

"He pulled the top of my dress down and his h-hands were in places I didn't want." Her voice hiccupped and she dropped her chin. "I kept telling him to stop, but he didn't l-listen. I don't know what would have happened if another car hadn't pulled in. It was a friend of mine, and I got a ride back with her and h-her date." She began to shake.

Rebecca reached across the table and took Melanie's icy hand. "Did you tell your parents?"

"N-no. I shouldn't have agreed to go to the lake. And maybe I gave Jack the w-wrong signal."

"No matter what signal you gave, no is no. If a guy doesn't respect that, it's on him. This wasn't your fault." She took a steadying breath. "Would you like me to call your parents? Ask them to come over? We can all talk about it together. They should know about this." Because someone needed to confront that boy's parents.

"I…I guess so."

Rebecca called them, and both her mother and father showed up. But when it became clear they didn't intend to do anything about what had happened, she sent Melanie to her office so she could speak with them in private.

Once they were alone, she gave them her most intimidating glare. "So you're going to let this boy get away with that behavior? He could have raped your daughter."

Her father flinched, then wiped a hand down his face. "We appreciate your concern, Ms. Matthews. And of course we want to protect Melanie. But Jack is the son of the plant manager, and my job is already in jeopardy. My wife has medical expenses, and I have four kids to support. I can't afford to make my boss mad. Besides, nothing happened."

Rebecca gritted her teeth. Breathed in through her nose. "Something *did* happen, Mr. Lewis. Melanie was traumatized last night. An incident like that can leave emotional scars that never heal. And retribution in the workplace is illegal."

"That doesn't stop it from happening, though." He stood, a slump of resignation in his shoulders. "We'll do our best to protect her from situations like this, and we'll keep her away from that boy. That's all we can do."

The three of them left, her parents flanking Melanie as they held her hands.

Clearly they cared about her.

But it was wrong to let that boy get away with what bordered on criminal behavior. What if that other car hadn't driven up and prevented him from finishing what he started?

A shudder rippled through her.

Melanie had been lucky to escape with her virtue intact.

But she could easily carry the emotional scars for the rest of her life.

Adrenaline pinging, Rebecca strode into the kitchen. She needed an outlet for all of the restless energy and anger coursing through her. And since cooking was her happy place, she was in the perfect spot.

So she'd bang pots and smash garlic and hack at vegetables until she calmed down.

However long that took.

* * *

Why was Rebecca's car at the restaurant late on a Sunday afternoon?

As Zach passed by the alley that ran behind the row of shops, he slowed.

This was out of pattern—but the timing couldn't have been better. Now that he'd dropped Isabel off at a slumber party with a new friend from Sunday school, his evening was free. And he and Rebecca needed to talk one-on-one, without little ears nearby. He couldn't say goodbye to Ste. Genevieve in three weeks when his leave expired without attempting to find out why she'd backed off from him.

He pulled in, parked beside Rebecca's car, and crossed toward the back door of the restaurant. Paused when the muted sounds of banging, clattering, and slamming seeped out.

Frowning, he started forward again.

From what he'd observed, Rebecca was a quiet cook. And she never worked at the restaurant on Sunday.

Who was in there?

He stopped at the door and gave a loud knock.

The noise inside continued.

He tried again.

If no one answered this time, he'd call 911 and—

The door was yanked open to reveal a glowering Rebecca.

As he took in her flushed face, clenched jaw, and the brackets of strain around her rigid mouth, his pulse accelerated. "Are you all right?"

"I'm fine." She snapped out the words. "What are you doing here? Where's Isabel?"

His alarm ratcheted up at her uncharacteristic bad humor. "I saw your car in the alley as I drove by. Isabel's at the sleepover we talked about."

"Oh. Right." She pushed back a few strands of hair that had escaped from her French braid.

"Why are you here on a Sunday?"

"I booked a luncheon for tomorrow when the restaurant is closed. Why do you care, anyway?" Irritation rolled off her in waves.

He tucked his fingers into his pockets and kept his voice

steady. "What's wrong, Rebecca?"

"Nothing." Even though her sharp tone said otherwise. "Can't a person put in a few extra hours at—" She stopped. Sniffed. Whipped around and raced back to the smoking pan on the stove. After grabbing it with a potholder, she dropped it into the stainless steel sink with a loud clatter. "Now see what you made me do? All those onions are ruined." Anger seethed from every pore in her body as her voice broke.

Whoa.

Something was seriously wrong.

Zach entered, even though she hadn't invited him in, propped a shoulder against the wall, and stayed out of her way.

As the pan sizzled in the sink, she turned to the carrots lying next to the cutting board and began to chop them with more force than necessary.

After a few minutes, she lasered him a glance. "I don't need an audience. Do you have something to say?"

"Yes. But I was giving you a chance to cool down first." He kept his tone mild—a gargantuan effort when his pulse was racing and every red alert in his body was going off.

She went back to chopping carrots.

"Are you angry at me, Rebecca?"

"No." Chop, chop, chop.

"You could have fooled me."

"Sorry." Chop, chop, chop.

"Well, you're obviously angry about something. Do you want to tell me what's wrong?"

Silence, except for the knife hitting the cutting board.

Just when he thought she was going to ignore him, she spoke. "Do you know Melanie Lewis? She's one of my high school servers."

"Yes. She's in my English lit classes. Why?"

"She went to the end-of-school dance last night with the son of her father's boss, and he attacked her." She hurled a handful of carrots into the bowl beside her.

Zach straightened up. Narrowed his eyes. "What do you mean by attacked?"

"Exactly what I said."

"Can you give me a few more details?"

"If you'll keep them to yourself."

"Goes without saying."

She launched into a recap of the incident, her voice shaking. "If that other car hadn't come by, this boy could be facing criminal charges."

"Is Melanie okay?"

"Physically, yes. Emotionally, I'm not certain. I talked to her parents about it, but they're not going to do anything. Can you believe that?" Anger flared in her irises.

He furrowed his brow. "I don't know how much they *could* do. Those types of situations can be sticky. You only heard one side of the story. Maybe it was a misunderstanding."

Rebecca stared at him. "A girl was practically raped and you call that a misunderstanding?"

"We haven't heard his side."

"I heard Melanie's, and I saw her eyes. She told him to back off, and he ignored her. She isn't lying about this."

"I didn't say she was. And I'm not saying she wasn't frightened." Zach tried for a placating tone. "But maybe he misinterpreted her cues."

"Or maybe he just decided to add another notch to his belt." Fury radiated from her. "There's no way to misinterpret a no."

"All I'm saying is that we don't know the whole story. A

charge like that could ruin a young man's life."

"What do you think it does to the victim's?" She was almost vibrating with rage.

This conversation was getting way too emotional.

"You did everything you could, Rebecca. You talked to Melanie. You talked to her parents. They made their decision. There's nothing else you can do."

In silence she finished chopping the carrots and moved on to celery.

He tried again. "There's a huge stigma attached to a charge like this, whether it's true or not. I did a series on date rape a couple of years ago, and it's a murky issue."

She looked at him, eyes blazing. "So Mr. Journalist thinks he's an expert because he wrote a few articles."

"It was an in-depth series." A touch of defensiveness crept into his voice. "As a matter of fact, it won an award."

"Well, excuse me. I guess that qualifies you as an expert." She attacked the celery with renewed vigor.

His own temper began to flare.

Planting his fists on his hips, he faced her across the counter. "I do know a thing or two about the subject. What makes *you* such an expert on the topic?"

She glared at him, one hand clenched around the knife, the other white-knuckled as it gripped the edge of the counter. When she spoke, her voice shook. "Because when I was Melanie's age, I came this close," she held up one trembling hand and measured a meager half-inch gap between her thumb and index finger, "to having it happen to me."

As her revelation reverberated in the sudden quiet between them, Zach sucked in a breath.

He'd wanted an explanation for her skittishness.

But now that she'd provided it, he was almost sorry she had.

Because it made him sick to his stomach.

He closed his eyes. Fisted his hands at his sides.

A sensitive, caring woman like Rebecca would be marred for life by such an experience. Whoever had pushed himself on her had taken what should have been a beautiful experience and made it an act of aggression, devoid of tenderness or even consideration.

No wonder a close encounter with a man who could easily overpower her would freak her out.

No wonder she was fearful when even a hint of passion surfaced.

No wonder she didn't date.

He slowly exhaled. Opened his eyes.

Just in time to see Rebecca waver. Grope for the counter. Start a slow nosedive toward the unforgiving edge of the stainless steel work island.

He lunged toward her, but despite her obvious dizziness she lurched back from him. "Don't touch me." She groped behind her for the stove, then wrapped her arms around her body as she leaned against it and stared at him with slightly unfocused eyes.

Her instruction had been clear, but he didn't want to follow it.

What he wanted to do was pull her into his arms and hold her until she felt safe and protected and loved.

But that's not how she'd feel if he moved forward.

She'd feel threatened.

So he stopped a few feet away, far enough to give her space but close enough to grab her if she started to pass out.

A shudder rippled through her, and he swallowed past the burning rage that was consuming him. Comfort and compassion, not anger, were what she needed now.

If she wouldn't let him go to her, maybe he could get her to come to him.

Slowly he lifted his hand and held it out. "Let me help, Rebecca."

She shook her head, her eyes suddenly flat and lifeless. "It's too late."

"I don't believe that."

"Believe it. You saw what happened when you kissed me."

"I didn't know your story then. If I had, my approach would have been different."

"The outcome would have been the same."

"I don't think so. And I think you owe it to yourself—to both of us—to test that theory."

"It doesn't matter, Zach." The rigid line of her shoulders collapsed. "You're going back to St. Louis soon."

"That's a manageable distance."

"You'll forget about me once you're immersed in your old life again."

"I would never forget you." He locked gazes with her, willing her to see the truth in what he was saying. "I think you and I have potential. And I think not exploring that would be a huge mistake. Sit with me in the restaurant. Let's talk. Please."

Indecision warred with a faint hint of hope on her face. "You could be wasting your time."

"I'll take that risk."

A few beats ticked by. "Give me five minutes to clean up in here and calm down. Then I'll meet you in the restaurant with my answer."

Tempted as he was to push for an affirmative response now, Zach refrained. Rebecca had asked for space, and he had to respect that.

So he lowered his hand and walked over to the door, pausing on the threshold before pushing through. “I promise you that I would never do anything to hurt you, Rebecca. And you can trust me to honor that promise.”

Then he pushed through the door, chose a table, and sat down to wait for her verdict.

12

As the door closed behind Zach, Rebecca filled her lungs. The waves of blackness that had crashed over her had receded, but her legs were too wobbly to be reliable.

She groped her way to the work island and slid onto a stool. The clean-up could wait until she felt more stable. At the moment she had more pressing matters to think about.

Like whether to share any more details of her history with Zach.

But really, at this point why hold back? She'd already spilled the core of her secret. And his compassionate, caring eyes said he'd respect and protect anything else she divulged.

She picked up a stray piece of celery from the counter and tossed it in the bowl with the rest of the chopped vegetables.

Could her problem be surmountable, as Zach seemed to think?

Unknown.

But if he was willing to work with her to try to overcome it, what did she have to lose—except an opportunity for love that might never come again?

Put like that, her decision was a no-brainer.

As soon as her legs were steady enough to support her, she gave the kitchen a fast clean-up and joined him in the restaurant.

He stood as she approached, eyeing her with a slight wariness. As if he was assessing her mental state and trying to figure out if she was going to go off the deep end again.

"I'm finished with the dramatics for the night. And I left all the knives in the kitchen, in case you're worried." It was a poor attempt at humor, but she needed to tamp down the tension in the air. "I also want to apologize for how I behaved when you arrived. It wasn't fair to take my anger and frustration out on you."

"I've been subjected to worse. And for a lot less reason."

"Thanks for being so gracious." She sat.

He took the chair at a right angle to hers. "I'm sure hearing Melanie's story today brought back terrible memories."

"It did. And I've never shared them with anyone. Not even what I let slip with you tonight."

His eyebrows rose. "You never told your family?"

"No."

He folded his hands on the table. "Sometimes talking about a bad experience can help put it to rest. I've been told I'm a decent listener—and my ear is available."

His measured tone, and the aura of protectiveness and safety and compassion he projected, enfolded her like a warm embrace. "Are you sure you have the time?"

"My evening is yours."

She looked down. Touched a stain on the linen tablecloth that would have to be dealt with before tomorrow. Swallowed. "I was sixteen. The same age as Melanie. I guess that's why her experience hit so close to home."

"Who was the boy?"

"The high school football hero. Everyone wanted to go out with him. I couldn't believe it when he asked me to the spring dance, which was the biggest social event of the season. For a first date, it was quite a coup."

Shock flattened Zach's features. "You mean this happened the very first time you ever went out?"

"Yes."

He muttered a word she couldn't make out, but it didn't sound pretty. "What did he do?"

"After the dance was over I agreed to go for a drive with him. I assumed he had some mild making-out on his mind, and I thought it would be exciting to have a first date and a first kiss all in the same night. Except he was after a lot more than kissing." Her voice faltered.

Zach extended his hand across the table. Inviting her to take it, but leaving the decision up to her.

After a moment she slipped her fingers into his, and he gave them a gentle squeeze. "We drove to Miller's Point. It wasn't the usual make-out place, but I figured he got around more than most of the guys and had scoped out a few off-the-beaten-path places." She swallowed past the bile that rose in her throat. "He had a bottle of wine in the car. I only drank one glass, but that was also a first for me and it had a big impact. After the wine, he said he knew a spot that overlooked the river, and suggested we sit there and enjoy the view. I said yes."

She began to shake, and Zach squeezed her hand again as his compelling gaze fused with hers. "It happened a long time ago, Rebecca. It can only hurt you now if you let it."

"I know." He was right in theory, if not in practice. But maybe after she got through this retelling, she'd be able to put the incident to rest once and for all. "For a few minutes it was fine. He kissed me, and it was nice. But all of a sudden, he morphed into a different person. He became really aggressive, and his kisses got rough. I started to get scared, and I tried to pull away. But he pushed me to the ground and lay on top of me. He was big and strong. My arms were pinned down and I-I couldn't move."

Zach didn't say a word, but a muscle in his jaw ticced and a leashed fury simmered in his eyes.

"I had long hair, and he twisted it in his hand so I couldn't move my head. The more I struggled, the harder he pulled." She squeezed her eyes shut for a moment, and a tear trailed down her cheek. "I fought as much as I could, but it was useless. I tried to scream, but he never took his lips off mine. There wouldn't have been anyone to hear me anyway in that remote spot."

Zach scooted his chair slightly closer and tightened his grip on her hand.

Her respiration was shorting out, but she was almost finished. She could get through this as long as she held on to him.

"All of a sudden I felt him p-pulling up my dress, and I heard a zipper. I…I knew what he was planning to do. I think I…I was hysterical by then, because I d-don't remember clearly what happened next. Except that out of the blue it started to pour. It was as if the heavens had opened—almost like a miracle. In any case, the rain dampened his enthusiasm and his determination, and he took off for the car."

"What did *you* do?"

"For a while I just lay there. I think I was in shock. But finally I got up and went back to the car. He was waiting for me, none too patiently, and he was beyond aggravated that his rented tux had gotten wet. I didn't want to get back in the car, but we were in the middle of nowhere and I figured it would be more dangerous to wander the back roads on foot in a storm. Besides, his interest had cooled. He took me home, and two weeks later he asked me out again—believe it or not."

Silence fell between them, broken only by the distant, muted whistle of a train.

When Zach at last spoke, his gentle tone was at odds with his taut posture and the anger in his eyes. "And you never told anyone about this?"

"No, I was too ashamed. I felt like maybe it was my fault, that I'd done something wrong, encouraged him in some way."

"You don't still think that, do you?"

"No. But it took me years to get past that. And I never did get over my fear of being alone with men. That's why the few dates I've been on were disasters. Every time a man invades my personal space my brain reads it as an attack. I know that's irrational, but I can't seem to control the panic. It overwhelms me. My freaked-out reaction scared my dates and embarrassed me. Needless to say, they never came back. And I wouldn't have gone out with them again if they had."

"Did you ever think about counseling?"

"Yes. But I was always too embarrassed to talk about what happened. I assumed time would take care of the problem, but it didn't."

"So you stopped dating."

"Yes."

He released a breath. "At least now I understand what happened on Easter. And that it wasn't a personal rejection."

"Far from it. It had nothing to do with you. But I can't control how I react, Zach. Touching makes me feel fear, not desire. And no man's ego can tolerate that forever."

He studied her for a moment. "You want my take? I don't think the right man's ego would *have* to tolerate it forever. And I think I'm that man. I've seen the way you look at me, Rebecca. I know there's passion in your heart. You're just afraid to let those feelings out. But my ego is strong enough to handle your fear until you feel comfortable enough to move forward, and I have infinite patience. I think you and I could have something very special, and I think you owe it to yourself—to both of us—to give this thing a chance."

She tried not to let the hope stirring to life in her heart take root. "You saw what happened when you kissed me. What if I freak out again?"

"You won't. Because now that I know your background, I'll follow your lead on pacing. Whatever is comfortable for you is fine with me. And by the way…touching doesn't bother you as much as you think."

She frowned. "Yes, it does."

"No, it doesn't." He lifted their linked fingers and stroked the side of her hand with his thumb. "Does this make you afraid?"

"No."

"So let's figure out what level of touching is acceptable." He reached over with his other hand and traced a gentle finger down her cheek. "How about this?"

She closed her eyes as a shiver of pleasure rippled through her. "I…I like that."

"Then let's try this." He kept his fingers twined with hers but placed his other hand flat on the table. Then he leaned over and brushed his lips across her forehead, lingering on her temple a moment before he drew back. "Did that scare you?"

"No." Just the opposite. It set off fireworks and awakened a hunger deep inside that stole the breath from her lungs. "That was nice."

"How about this?" He skimmed his fingers over her lips, whisper-soft, then cupped her cheek with his palm.

She sighed and leaned into his strong fingers. "I like that a lot. But that won't be enough for you. Not for very long, anyway."

"Yes, it will. I told you. I'm a patient man." He leaned back but maintained his hold on her hand. "Here's my suggestion. We'll take this a day at a time, and we'll have one simple rule. If I touch you in a way you don't like, tell me and I'll stop. Over time, as you get more at ease with the physical side of our relationship, I think your comfort level for touching will expand. But I'll follow your cues on that, and I'll announce my intentions if I'd like to get close. Does that work for you?"

He was being so accommodating and understanding—how could she refuse to give his plan a try when every fiber of her being yearned to make a relationship with this special man work?

"Yes."

The warmth of his smile sent her pulse into the stratosphere. "Thank you for that. And for your trust. I won't betray it." He squeezed her hand again, then released it. "Are you finished here?"

"Yes."

"I'll walk you out."

He followed her to the kitchen, waited while she shut everything down for the night and locked the door, then strolled beside her in the balmy night air to her car.

At the driver-side door, he waited while she unlocked it and tossed her purse onto the passenger seat. When she straightened up and turned to him, his lips bowed again. "So here's an example of how this will work. Right now, I'd like to kiss you. But observe." He slid his hands into his pockets and took a step back, giving her space. "A simple touch of lips, no hands, plenty of room between us. Is that okay?"

For an experienced man who no doubt could have his pick of women eager to share his bed if not his life, his infinite sensitivity and consideration only intensified her feelings for him.

"Yes."

True to his word, the kiss he gave her was sweet, simple—and potent.

On her end, anyway.

But surely for him it was less than adequate.

When he backed off, she took a steadying breath. "I liked that, Zach. A lot. But I doubt it's anywhere close to enough for you."

"It is for now. And I have great confidence it will lead to more in time."

"I wish I was as sure about that as you seem to be."

"Trust me on this." He backed up. "I'll wait until you drive away."

She slid behind the wheel, started the engine, and put the car in gear.

When she reached the end of the alley, she glanced in her rearview mirror.

Zach was standing where she'd left him, hands still in his pockets.

But if all went well…if his confidence proved justified…one of these days those hands would come out and work magic between the two of them.

Though that prospect set off a tiny flutter of alarm in her nerve endings, she had a feeling that if he was as patient as he promised to be, his perseverance would end up paying amazing dividends.

For both of them.

* * *

Zach slid the final papers from his desk into his briefcase, snapped the clasp shut, and gave the deserted classroom a slow scan.

It was hard to believe the last day of school had already arrived.

"Mr. Wright?"

Zach glanced toward the door and smiled. "Hi, Pete."

"Do you have a minute?"

"Sure. Come on in. I thought everyone had cleared out by now."

"I was just cleaning out my locker." But that mundane activity hadn't produced the slight flush on his cheeks, the spark in his eyes, or the excitement radiating from him.

"What's up?"

A grin spread across his face. "I won the short story contest."

Zach blinked. "You mean you're the national winner?"

"Yeah. The story will be published next fall. And there's a thousand-dollar prize."

His lips bowed. "That's fantastic. Congratulations." He gave the boy's fingers a firm shake. "I knew you could do it. You have tremendous talent."

A flush spread over his cheeks. "If it hadn't been for you, this would never have happened."

Zach shook his head. "It's hard to hide talent like yours, Pete. Sooner or later you would have found your voice, with or without me."

"I don't think so, Mr. Wright. I was at kind of a low point in my life, getting involved in some things that weren't…well…very good. But you made me believe in myself. I wouldn't even have known about the contest if it hadn't been for you. So I just wanted to say thanks for making a difference in my life. And to ask if it would be okay for me to keep in touch when you go back to St. Louis."

"I'd be disappointed if you didn't. And I'll be in town for

another two weeks."

"Maybe I'll run into you at Ms. Matthews' restaurant."

"Count on it."

"Well...I gotta run. See you around."

As Zach watched Pete disappear out the door, a sense of deep contentment settled over him.

Never in all his years of reporting had he been aware of making such a direct impact on a single life.

And it felt good. Very good.

He propped a hip on the edge of the desk, folded his arms, and gazed out the window at the lush spring foliage.

When he'd arrived in Ste. Genevieve, the mid-February world had been gray and dead and cold. Now it was bright and alive and warm.

Like his heart.

For here, in this small rural town, he'd found work that energized him in a way journalism no longer did. He'd found, through Isabel, a new outlook on the world and discovered a surprising paternal side to his personality. And he'd found a woman to love, whose heart was awakening like tulips responding to the warmth of the spring sun, as her brother had referenced in his Easer sermon.

The corner of his mouth rose another notch.

In the two short weeks since she'd shared her story with him, their relationship had made tremendous progress. Much more than he could ever have hoped for. She'd relaxed with him, even initiating an occasional tentative touch that filled him with delight.

The two of them were going to be fine. He knew that as surely as he knew she was one in a million. Heck, he'd propose to her tomorrow if he thought she was ready for that step. But one day soon, hopefully in the not-too-distant future, she *would* be ready.

Now all he had to decide was whether to accept the offer at the high school or stick with journalism and resign himself to a very long commute.

The drive would be worth it, though, as long as he could share his life with Rebecca and—

His phone began to vibrate, and he pulled it out. Scanned the screen.

Huh.

Ted Larsen typically confined his communication to texts and emails.

He put the phone to his ear and greeted the managing editor.

As usual, the man got straight to business after a cursory hello. "I have some news. I'd prefer to do this in person, but since you won't be back in town for a couple of weeks a call will have to suffice. Joe Adams has decided to take early retirement. We're sorry to see him go, to be honest. He's done a fine job as Washington Bureau chief. But new blood won't hurt. The job is yours if you want it."

Zach's jaw dropped.

They wanted him to be Washington Bureau chief?

That was the most coveted job on the newspaper. A chance to mingle with the movers and shakers in the nation's capital, to do in-depth coverage of the events that shaped the country. Press conferences with the president. Interviews with the secretary of state. Access to the most powerful political figures in the world.

Wow.

"You still there?" Ted sounded amused.

"Yes." Somehow he found his voice. "To say I'm overwhelmed would be a gross understatement."

"You shouldn't be that surprised. You're a top-notch reporter. You deserve this promotion. You interested?"

Of course he was interested.

But there were complications now that hadn't been there a few weeks ago. New perspectives. A shift in priorities.

And a woman who'd stolen his heart.

"Am I picking up hesitation?"

At Ted's question, he cleared his throat. "It's just…a lot to take in." And evaluate.

Because Rebecca wouldn't like the fast-paced, glitzy life in Washington, even if she loved him enough to go. The quieter, simpler small-town ambiance suited her. And it suited him too, as long as she was by his side.

"Why don't you take a few days to think it over? But remember—opportunities like this don't come along very often."

That was true.

Yet as they ended the call and Zach gathered up his belongings, another truth echoed in his mind.

While opportunities like the offer of Washington Bureau chief were rare, others only came along once in a lifetime.

Like winning the love of the most wonderful woman he'd ever met.

And even though the Washington job would be exciting and offer him the forum to do some of the best reporting of his life, he'd also have to give up a lot. The opportunity to have a direct, positive impact on young people's lives as a teacher. A lifestyle that gave him time to breathe. And not too far down the road, if all went well, a chance to create—with the woman he loved—a home and family that would sustain him all the days of his life.

Bottom line, the excitement of the Washington job would fade in time, and in the end all he'd have to show for his adventure in the nation's capital would be a dusty scrapbook of stories and perhaps a few awards to hang on his wall. Tangible reminders of success that had been bought at a high price—the life he could have had in Ste. Genevieve.

Put in those terms, his decision was easy.

But much depended on Rebecca.

So even though it was too soon to ask for a firm commitment from her, he needed to share this news, get her thoughts on what the future might hold—and hope her vision meshed with his.

And he needed to do it ASAP.

He strode to his car and headed to the restaurant to pick up Isabel, but when he arrived the place was a zoo.

"What's going on?" He tossed the question to Rose as she whizzed by and Isabel gathered up her things.

"Crazy day." She rolled her eyes. "We had a large group come for a late lunch, and they're still out there. That makes it hard to get ready for the Friday night dinner crowd. We're trying to hurry them along, but so far no luck. Rebecca's out there now doing her best to diplomatically suggest they wind down their gathering."

As Rose bustled over to the refrigerator, Rebecca pushed through the door, looking frazzled. When she saw him, though, she summoned up a smile. "Welcome to the nuthouse."

"Rose filled me in. We'll get out of your hair. But when you have a spare minute, let me know. I have something to talk with you about."

"You know how busy my weekends are. Is it important?"

Yeah, it was. But he needed her undivided attention when they talked, and she was busy sunup to sundown on Fridays and Saturdays.

"It can wait. Why don't we plan on a picnic Sunday?"

She squinted at him. "That would be lovely, but can you give me a clue about the subject matter of our discussion?"

Hmm.

Maybe that wasn't a bad idea.

He angled away from the kitchen bustle and lowered his voice. "I have two job offers."

Her eyebrows peaked. "What kind of offers?"

"A teaching slot at the high school in the fall and Washington Bureau chief for my paper."

She blinked. "Wow."

"I had the same reaction."

"What are you going to do?"

"Nothing until we talk." He reached for her hand. Squeezed her fingers. "Your input is key to my decision."

"Rebecca, one of the men in the dawdling party is complaining his soup is cold." Frances hurried over. "I told him that's how vichyssoise is supposed to be served, but he's not buying it. Could you talk to him?"

"Of course. Zach, I'm sorry, but—"

"We're out of here. We'll talk Sunday." He rounded up Isabel and exited through the back door as second thoughts began messing with his mind.

Springing the news on her like that hadn't been ideal in many ways.

Still, it was probably more fair to give her a chance to mull it over before they talked.

When they did, however, he intended to make his intentions absolutely clear—and hope she was as convinced as he was that the two of them had a future together.

* * *

Rebecca removed her apron, brushed some stray strands of hair back from her face, and blew out a breath.

What a weekend.

Friday had been crazy, but today had been worse. Being short one server for Saturday lunch was bad enough, but when Rose started feeling poorly and left early, there'd been no one to do all the mise en place duties for dinner—on top of all the cooking—except yours truly.

It hadn't helped that she'd been distracted ever since Zach shared his news yesterday, either.

She hung up her apron. Wiped a spot off the pristine stainless steel counter.

Of course she was happy for him. The Washington offer was a career coup.

But a teaching job would never be able to compete with it.

So he'd take the DC position. After all, he'd spent his whole journalism career working toward such a prestigious job.

And that was bad news for the two of them.

Maintaining a long-distance relationship between St. Louis and Ste. Genevieve was manageable, but it was far less feasible if he lived almost a thousand miles away.

That's probably why he'd invited her on the picnic. To tell her he was leaving.

Shoulders sagging, she trudged across the kitchen to retrieve her purse.

In truth, it was hard to blame him for that choice. The opportunity was too good to pass up. Washington offered glitz, glamour, prestige, recognition, and a higher profile for his work. All she had to offer was her love—but there was no guarantee when or if she'd be able to give full physical expression to it.

Under Zach's gentle, patient nurturing, she'd made great strides in a short time, but he deserved more than simple kisses.

He was the type of man who would approach the physical component of love with joy, giving affection without inhibition. And he had every right to expect the same from a partner.

Problem was, she might never get there.

She picked up her purse and fished out her keys.

Bottom line?

When weighing the guaranteed excitement of Washington and the challenge of working in the nation's capital in a prestigious position against taking a chance on a woman who might never be able to fully express her love, it was no contest.

So much for all the hopes she'd begun to harbor that—

Her phone began to trill as she reached up to flick off the lights, and her pulse stuttered.

No one would call her at eleven-thirty unless there was an emergency.

She groped through her purse until her fingers closed over her cell. Pulled it out and scanned the screen.

Zach.

Not good.

She put the phone to her ear. "What's wrong?"

"Are you still at the restaurant?"

"Yes."

"I know it's late, but can you come over?"

Her stomach knotted. "Is Isabel okay?"

"Yes. She's asleep. I just had an email from a friend of Josef's. He's—" His voice choked, and she tightened her grip on the receiver as a feeling of foreboding swept over her. When he spoke again she hardly recognized his shattered voice. "Josef is dead."

13

As Zach's shocking news slowly registered in her numb brain, Rebecca's legs turned to rubber and she groped for a stool. Sank onto it. "Oh, Zach." The room blurred and a tear leaked out of her eye.

"Can you come over?"

It wasn't a question. It was an SOS.

"I'll be there in five minutes."

Fingers trembling, she ended the call and extracted her keys. Stood. Clung to the edge of the counter until her legs steadied.

Once behind the wheel, she drove as fast as she dared through the quiet, dark streets.

The minute she pulled up in front of Zach's apartment he opened the door.

After setting the brake, she hurried up the walk, his haggard, grief-ravaged face knotting her stomach. The instant he closed the door behind her, she tossed her purse on the couch and wrapped her arms around him.

He buried his face in her shoulder, shudders rippling through him as he clung to her like a drowning man holding tight to a life preserver.

When he at last drew back, she reached up and laid a hand against his cheek. "I'm so sorry."

"Me too." His words were choked. "He was such a good

man. The kind the world needs more of. Caring, compassionate, committed. Why would God allow someone like him to die?"

It was the age-old question that had no answer.

"I don't know." She took his hand. "What happened? Who contacted you?"

"Josef apparently asked a colleague named Stefan to notify me if—" His voice broke, and he swallowed. "Stefan said Josef was working late at their makeshift office, and that a bomb went off inside. He was…killed instantly."

A wave of nausea swept over her. "This feels like a terrible nightmare."

"Tell me about it." He motioned toward the coffee table. "I got that out of the closet, but I haven't been able to bring myself to open it."

Rebecca glanced at the large envelope addressed in Josef's hand to Zach. The one that had been packed in Isabel's luggage, with instructions to open it only if something like this happened. "Maybe it will be easier if we do it together."

"That's one of the reasons I asked you to come over tonight. I couldn't face that alone."

He led her to the couch, and she sat beside him as he picked up the envelope, slit the edge with shaky fingers, and slid the contents onto his lap.

There were a number of items inside, held together with a large rubber band, but she leaned close as he angled the letter on top toward her so they could read it together.

My dear Zachary,

If you are reading this, it is because I have been called home to God. Please do not grieve for me, my friend. I am at peace, and I am once more with my beloved Katrina. All is well with me.

It is Isabel, not me, who needs your sympathy. In recent weeks, it has become clear to me that without her mother or me here to watch over her, my country will be an inhospitable place for her. It is filled with strife and terror, and while I still believe that will change, I do not think it will happen during her youth. So there is no life here, no future, for my precious child.

Therefore, Zachary, it is my final wish that Isabel remain in America, the country of her birth, which was always so good to me. I do not expect you to take on the responsibility of raising her. I would not stretch the bounds of our friendship that far. But I do ask that you find her a good and loving home. I have great faith that you will do your best to make sure she is happy and loved.

In this envelope you will find all of the necessary papers—records of Isabel's birth and baptism, of my marriage to Katrina and of her death, as well as letters from my family and my minister, who support my decision. Very soon Stefan will send you a record of my death as well. Should you need to obtain any other records or letters, he has agreed to assist you. I have enclosed his contact information.

I have also included some things for Isabel. Letters her mother and I wrote to each other, photos of her relatives and the house where we lived, some pages from my journal. I want her to make a new life in America, but it is also important for her to remember her roots.

My dear Zachary, you have my deepest gratitude for all you have already done for Isabel. I hope you will forgive me for placing this one last obligation on you. But I hope the bond we share will make my request less burdensome. You are my brother in everything but blood—and I could not have chosen a finer man to fill that role.

I know that this is a difficult time for you. Separation is always painful. But please do not grieve too deeply. I have had a good, full life. I have done satisfying, worthwhile work. I have known the great joy of fatherhood. And I have loved—and been loved—by a woman beyond compare. No man can ask for more.

So farewell, my friend, until we meet again. And know that you will always be in my prayers.

The words blurred as Rebecca finished the letter, and when she looked at Zach his face was a mask of grief.

The silence between them as he clung to her hand was broken only by the muted patter of rain outside as the dark clouds that had been hovering all day released their stored-up moisture.

At last Zach swiped the back of his hand across his damp lashes and took a shuddering breath. "I respected Josef more than any man I've ever met. I know he accepted this possibility, made his peace with it, but it's not as easy for me. And Isabel will be devastated. Not only is her father gone, but she has no home to return to. She's going to be so lost." His words were ragged.

Yes, she was.

Unless…

An idea began to take shape in Rebecca's mind, so out-of-the-blue her pulse lost its rhythm.

The whole notion was crazy.

Wasn't it?

Or was it inspired instead?

Because it felt right. And good. And meant to be.

Zach might not agree. He might even try to talk her out of it.

But sometimes you had to listen to your heart.

* * *

"Zach."

At Rebecca's touch on his arm, Zach turned to her. Frowned.

An odd energy was radiating from her. Hard as he tried to identify it—nervousness…excitement…anxiety…anticipation…yearning….hope—he failed.

"What's wrong?"

"Nothing. At least not in the way you mean. I'm just thinking about Isabel." She caught her lower lip between her teeth for a moment. "The thing is—I'd like to take her. I've grown to love her over these past few weeks, and I can't bear the thought of sending her off to live with strangers. I realize a single-parent household isn't ideal, but I'd do my best to give her enough love to make up for the absence of a father."

Pressure built behind his eyes as she finished.

What an amazing woman.

If he wasn't already in love, her sincere, compassionate, generous offer would have pushed him over the edge.

And in a way, it did.

Because all at once he ditched his plan to hold off on proposing to her until she was more comfortable with the physical component of marriage.

Taking a steadying breath, he wove his fingers with hers. "Maybe it doesn't have to be a single-parent household."

Her breath hitched. "What do you mean?"

He filled his lungs. "She'd have two parents if we got married."

She blinked. "Is that a…a proposal?"

"Yes. I realize this isn't an optimal moment for that, but fate seems to be pushing me to speed up my timetable."

"Because Isabel needs a dad."

What?

How could she think he only wanted to marry her for his goddaughter's sake?

Apparently his well-intentioned restraint had sent the wrong message about the depth of his feelings.

"No." He took both her hands, angled toward her, and locked onto her gaze. "I'm asking you to marry me because I love you. And *I* need *you*. I've been trying not to rush you, but sooner is better as far as I'm concerned. Because I can't imagine my life without you anymore."

Warmth filled her eyes—but so did a hint of doubt and trepidation. "What about the Washington job?"

"A year ago I would have jumped at it. But since then I've found something better. Life in Washington couldn't hold a candle to influencing young lives as a teacher and spending every day with the woman I love. A woman who captured my heart with her compassion and gentleness and warmth and sensitivity and kindness and intelligence and a hundred other qualities I could mention. I feel blessed beyond measure that you came into my life. Please say you'll marry me."

A tear slipped past her lashes, and she swiped it away. "I

want to say yes, but I'm so afraid I'll disappoint you. That I'll never be able to respond in the way you deserve."

"First of all, I have only one expectation if you agree to marry me. That you love me with all your heart—and for all time. And I've seen the passion your eyes. It's there, waiting for release. That will come in time."

"How can you be so certain? I've lived with this problem for years. My fear and panic over closeness won't go away overnight."

"I don't expect them to."

"But what if they never do?"

He took her hand, choosing his words with care. "The physical side of marriage would only be a small part of our life together. Most of the time it's about being there for each other in a thousand small ways, day in and day out. Those are the moments that make a union endure and grow stronger as the years pass.'

"But the physical side is important."

"Yes, it is." He wouldn't pretend otherwise. "So if the issue persists, we can try counseling. But this is what I know. I love you, and I want to spend my life with you. We can work out the rest as we go along."

"Are you sure about this?" Caution warred with hope in her eyes.

"I've never been more sure of anything—as long as you love me too."

"I do. With all my heart. I just don't want you to have any regrets about—"

"Can I have a glass of water, Uncle Zach?"

At the question from the doorway, Rebecca sucked in a breath and his stomach bottomed out.

They hadn't even talked about how best to break the tragic

news to the little girl they'd both come to love.

He glanced at Rebecca, who looked as panicked as he felt.

"Why are you here, Becca?" Isabel yawned and rubbed her eyes. "Is it morning already?"

"Not yet, sweetie." Rebecca's grip on his hand tightened.

Isabel looked back and forth between them, brow puckering. "What's wrong?"

The ability of kids to pick up nuances was a force to be reckoned with.

Taking a deep breath, Zach released Rebecca's hand, scooted over to make room for Isabel between them, and patted the sofa. "Come on in, honey. Rebecca and I have something to tell you."

Keeping a tight grip on her Raggedy Ann doll, she approached slowly, like a fawn that sensed danger. Expression solemn, she climbed onto the couch. "Is my papa sick?"

Zach took her small hand in his. "I got an email tonight from a friend of his." His heart began to pound so hard it was almost painful. "He had some bad news for us. Isabel, honey, your papa is…he isn't…I don't —" His voice turned to gravel.

Rebecca stepped in. "Sweetie, what Uncle Zach is trying to say is that your papa is…that he…he went to heaven."

The color seeped out of Isabel's face. "You mean he died? Like Mama?"

"Yes." Rebecca's reply was a broken whisper. "We're so sorry that—"

"No!" Isabel pulled her hand free and clutched the doll against her chest, her expression fierce. "I don't believe it. My papa wouldn't leave me alone. He promised he'd always take care of me."

"And he will." Zach stepped back in. "Remember the note he sent you on your birthday? About always being close to you in your heart, even when he was far away? He still is, honey. He'll always love you. It was just his time to go to heaven."

Her lower lip began to quiver, and a tear tracked down her cheek. "I want my Papa." As she started to cry, Rebecca pulled her onto her lap, tucked her close and smoothed her hair, murmuring reassurances as her anguished gaze met his over the top of Isabel's head.

Zach eased closer to them in the silent apartment, stroking Isabel's arm until at last her racking sobs subsided into a quiet snuffle.

"What-what will h-happen to me n-now?" Her choked question was muffled against Rebecca's shoulder. "I was supposed to go h-home next week. Where will I l-live?"

Zach nodded at Rebecca over Isabel's head, letting her take the lead while he held his breath and hoped she gave the answer he longed to hear.

Warmth filled her eyes, and peace settled over her countenance as she shifted her focus to Isabel. "You'll live with us"

Thank you, God.

Zach's lungs kicked back, and he closed the distance between them, draped his arm around her shoulders, and pulled them both close. "Would you like that, Isabel?"

She eased back a few inches so she could see both of them, her face splotchy and tear-stained. "You mean…stay here?"

"Yes. Rebecca and I are going to get married, and we want you to be part of our family."

Isabel's forehead crinkled. "Are you getting married because of me?"

"No, sweetie." Rebecca spoke before he could respond, her focus on him. "We would have gotten married anyway. Because we love each other." Then she shifted her attention to the little girl. "But it will be even better if you come to live with us."

Isabel bit her lower lip, face pensive. "I think my papa and mama would like me to do that." She turned to him. "I heard Papa say once that he wished you had someone like Mama and me to come home to. He said that would make you very happy. Now you have me and Becca. Does that make you happy, Uncle Zach?"

A hard question to answer in the midst of sadness.

But beneath his grief, there was, indeed, joy—along with a deep sense of contentment. And homecoming.

For while his path to love had been more circuitous than Josef's, he'd arrived at the same destination in the end. One he would treasure all the days of his life.

He reached down and touched Isabel's nose. Looked into Rebecca's beautiful, loving eyes. Smiled. "Yes, Isabel. It makes me happy to have you and Rebecca to come home to. For always."

* * *

"All right, let's get organized." Sam planted her hands on her hips as she surveyed the group assembled in the bride's room. "Henry, straighten your boutonniere. Isabel, don't play with your flowers or the petals might fall off. Rebecca, kindly descend from the clouds long enough to sit down so I can pin your veil on."

Rebecca smiled at Sam as she sat. How had she ever lucked out and gotten such a great sister-in-law? "I'm glad *someone's* in charge. My mind isn't on logistics today."

"Nor should it be. Brides have other priorities." Sam anchored the veil, fluffed the yards of whisper-soft tulle that drifted down the back, then urged her up and turned her to face the full-length mirror. "Now that's a bride."

Rebecca stared at her reflection.

Was that woman with the radiant face and shining eyes really her?

It all seemed too good to be real.

She touched the tulle, which floated over the waves of russet hair she'd worn loose and full for the occasion, in the style Zach preferred. Ran her fingers over the beading on the lace bodice of her white gown. Inhaled the scent of the roses from the bouquets.

"I guess it's real, isn't it?"

Sam snorted. "You better believe it's real, kiddo. And if you have any doubts, go ask that handsome man who's waiting for you at the altar." She turned to the audience of two watching the proceedings and angled her toward them. "Ladies and gentlemen, I give you the future Mrs. Zachary Wright."

Henry grinned. "I always knew you'd be a beautiful bride, Rebecca. Course, I just about gave up. But the day I met Zach, I had a feeling he was the one for you."

"You look pretty." Isabel reached out to touch the veil, her expression awed.

"Thank you, sweetie." Rebecca pointed to the brooch cradled in the little girl's palm. "Would you like me to pin that on for you?"

"Yes, please."

She knelt down. "I'm glad you wanted to wear this today." She secured it to the front of Isabel's tea-length dress, a duplicate of Sam's. "It makes me feel like your mama and papa are here with us."

"Me too." Isabel pressed her hand against the brooch. "Right by my heart."

The organ music changed, signaling the start of the ceremony, and a surge of sweet excitement swept over Rebecca as she stood.

Sam handed out the bouquets. "Do you remember everything we practiced last night, Isabel?"

"Yes."

"Good girl. Knock 'em dead, Rebecca." Sam gave her a thumbs-up and a wink, then took Isabel's hand as the two of them exited.

She watched them leave, then turned to her father with a tremulous smile. "I guess this is it, Dad."

"Yep." He cleared his throat. Dipped his chin and rocked forward onto the balls of his feet, hands clasped behind his back. "I'm mighty happy for you, Becca. Zach is a fine man. I'm only sorry your mother couldn't be here today. I know she'd offer you better words of wisdom than I can if she was. But I hope you and Zach have as wonderful a partnership as your mom and I did. Just remember that marriage is like a roller coaster. It has lots of ups and downs, but if you stay on track everything ends up fine. And don't forget to enjoy the ride."

"Thanks, Dad. For everything."

A sheen appeared in his irises, and he sniffed. "You ready for the big walk?"

"Yes." She slid her arm through his.

"Mighty pretty flowers." He examined her bouquet of white roses and pink tulips. "They make me think of spring."

"Me too." The very reason she'd chosen them.

Not typical for a Thanksgiving wedding—and expensive, since tulips were out of season—but they were the perfect flower for her, with all the symbolism Brad had spoken about so eloquently on Easter.

As she and her dad began the slow march down the aisle, faces beamed all around her. Rose and Frances, Ben, Pete and Melanie, Laura and Nick with their own new daughter. And Brad, waiting in front to perform the ceremony that would join her and Zach for life.

But it was Zach who drew—and held—her attention.

He looked incredibly handsome in his tux, of course. Strong. Solid. Steadfast.

But as Henry placed her hand in his and Zach smiled down at her, it was his eyes that held her spellbound. Filled with tenderness and love and yearning, they spoke more eloquently than words of the depth of his love.

And as they moved forward together, joy overflowed in her heart.

For never in her wildest dreams had she imagined that someday a man with such infinite patience would enter her life and create a bond of trust that had not only banished her fears but also unlocked the passion deep in her heart.

And for every day she and Zach were blessed to share, she'd give thanks for the miracle of his love that had made all her dreams come true.

Epilogue

Six months later

"Hey, sleepyhead, are you going to stay in bed all day?"

As Zach's teasing question nudged her awake, Rebecca kept her eyes closed and snuggled deeper under the sheet. "Maybe. Since Isabel's spending the weekend with Dad, we can get up anytime we want—or not. Want to join me?" She flung the sheet back invitingly, opened her eyes, and shifted toward him.

Froze.

He was carrying a tray holding a bud vase that contained two pink tulips, a plate of croissants, butter, jam, a pot of coffee, and eating utensils, and he was wearing a bow tie above his bare chest and sweat pants.

"What's all this?"

He deposited the tray on the nightstand, stuck his head in the closet, and removed two wrapped packages. "The magic must be wearing off already if you forgot the significance of the date." He joined her on the bed.

Warmth filled her, and her lips curved up. "I'd never forget our six-month anniversary. But most men don't remember those kinds of things."

Eyes softening, he leaned over to touch her cheek. "I guess I'm not most men—at least when it comes to you." His voice grew husky. "I've treasured each moment of our marriage and counted my blessings every single day." He stretched out beside her, propped his head on one hand, and reached over to play with the spaghetti strap of her gown.

Her throat constricted. "I'm the most blessed one in this relationship. I doubt many men would have exhibited your patience with such a skittish bride. Which I taxed to the limit in the early days of our marriage."

"Good things are worth waiting for." His irises darkened. "And since we overcame the hurdles, it's been very, very good."

A delicious tingle of anticipation swept over her as she leaned closer. "If I live a hundred years, I will never, ever take you for granted, Zach Wright. I love you more than words can say. Happy anniversary." She pressed her lips to his.

His response, as always, was instantaneous and all-consuming, leaving her breathless—and wanting more.

At last he drew back a bit and motioned to the presents. "If we keep this up, we may not get around to those—or the picnic we have planned for later."

"I don't mind if you don't." She snuggled closer.

A chuckle rumbled deep in his chest. "What have I unleashed?"

"Are you complaining?" She nibbled on his jaw.

"Never. But if you don't open those presents I may forget all about them."

She gave a dramatic sigh. "Fine. As long as we can get back to this fast."

"I'm on board with that."

She scooted into a more upright position while he remained propped on his side. When she tore the wrapping off the first package and removed the lid from the small box, her eyes misted.

"This is beautiful." She lifted the gold tulip on a delicate chain.

"That will always be our flower—a symbol of new life and new beginning after a long, dark winter." His voice was quiet now, and serious.

"You were my sun, you know." She feathered a kiss across his forehead. "Until you came along, I was only half living. Your warmth is what brought my heart to life. I love you so much sometimes it hurts."

He took her hand and pressed a tender kiss to her palm. "It's mutual, sweetheart. Go ahead and open the other one." He held out a flat package.

She pulled off the paper to find an envelope. At the return address, her heart skipped a beat. "Is this what I think it is?"

"Yes. It came yesterday, but I decided to keep it for today."

Fingers trembling, she opened the envelope and scanned the papers. Pressed them to her heart.

It was official.

Isabel was theirs.

She set both gifts aside and stretched out beside him, contentment settling over her like a cozy blanket on a chilly night. "It feels like we're truly a family now."

"I know what you mean." He played with a strand of her hair. "I thought breakfast in bed would help us celebrate. But we don't have to eat right away." He eased closer.

"We can delay breakfast…but I do have a present for you too."

He nuzzled her neck. "I can wait."

"Humor me and open it first." Because then they'd have even more to celebrate.

After a moment he backed off. "Only because I love you so much."

"I'll be right back." She scooted to the edge of the bed and stood. "Don't go anywhere."

"Never. You're stuck with me for life."

Blessed was more like it.

And as she hurried down the hall to retrieve her gift, she gave thanks.

For the man who'd walked with her step by stumbling step on the path to love, whose patient nurturing had healed her heart, and whose generous spirit and boundless kindness, compassion, and integrity would fill her world with light and joy all the days of her life.

* * *

Life didn't get any better than this.

Smiling, Zach stretched out flat on the bed and folded his hands on his stomach.

A perfect wife, a perfect daughter, a perfect job, a perfect home.

For a guy who'd lived on the adrenaline rush of investigative reporting, who'd always relegated love and family life to the back burner, who'd relished the fast pace of big-city living, it was amazing how content he was in this small river town.

Thanks to Rebecca. And Isabel. And work that fed his soul.

Who would ever have guessed that being assigned to cover a flood would lead him to a whole new, and better, life?

As Brad had said in his sermon at their wedding, God sometimes worked in mysterious ways to bring people together who could add light and joy to each other's lives.

Rebecca reentered, looking oh-so-sexy in her silky little sleep slip.

As for her tantalizing tousled hair?

It was soon going to be much more tousled.

She rejoined him on the bed and held out a small box, her eyes sparkling. "Happy anniversary. And don't spend five minutes feeling it and shaking it while you try to guess what's inside, like you did at Christmas."

"That's half the fun of presents." He grinned at her. "But since I have other things on my agenda today, I'll hurry this along." He waggled his eyebrows at her, then tore off the wrapping. From the flat box inside he extracted a picture frame with two openings. The latest shot of Isabel was on the left, but the other side was empty.

Huh.

Kind of a strange anniversary gift.

Unless she was planning to add a picture of the two of them to the other side?

"Very nice." He called up a smile as he tapped the empty slot. "Do you have another picture to go in here?"

"Not yet. But I do have some news."

"I'm not in the news game anymore." He reached over to finger her soft hair again.

"I think you'll want to hear this news."

"Can it wait?" He set the frame aside and leaned over to trail soft kisses along her collarbone.

"I suppose so. But I think a man whose wife was going to have a baby would want to know right away."

He froze. Lifted his head to stare at her as he digested the news. "A baby?"

"Mm-hm. You know—those little beings that cry and sleep and wet a lot." Her mouth curved up.

A baby.

They were going to have a baby!

Joy bubbled up inside him, more heady than the champagne they'd toasted with at their wedding.

"Wow." He cupped her face with his hands as the wonder of her news settled in. "When did you find out?"

"Yesterday. I didn't want to say anything until I was sure." She studied him. "I know it happened faster than either of us expected, but I hoped you'd be as thrilled as I am."

"I'm beyond thrilled. This is totally rad, as my students would say." He smiled at her, taking in every nuance of her beautiful, expressive features. "Do you have any idea how much I love you?"

"Why don't you show me?" She scooted closer, until only a whisper separated them.

He didn't need a second invitation.

And as he gathered her into his arms and lowered his lips to hers, gratitude infused his soul. For without this special woman, he might never have discovered the one simple truth Josef had always understood—that love is the only thing that really matters in the end.

And for a fleeting moment, just before he lost himself in the wonder of Rebecca's sweet love, he hoped Josef knew how things had turned out.

Because he had a feeling his friend would approve.

Keep reading for a preview of THE WAY HOME, Book 1 in the Family Ties series.

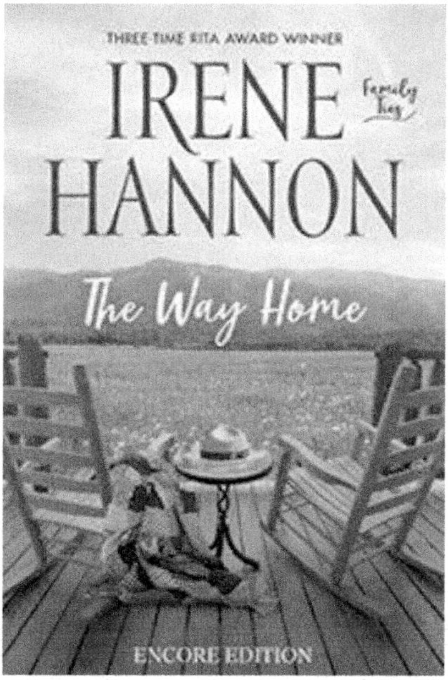

~Excerpt~

The Way Home

FAMILY TIES—BOOK 1

ENCORE EDITION

1

"Your target has arrived."

At the camera operator's alert, Amy Winter turned in the direction he was pointing and scanned the group of people milling about in front of the courthouse. "Where?"

"Straight ahead. Tall, dark hair, gray suit, intimidating. Carrying a black briefcase."

It took her only a moment to spot the assistant prosecuting attorney—and the term intimidating was spot-on. As he strode through the group of people clustered on the sidewalk and toward the door, his bearing communicated a clear back-off message.

A message she intended to ignore.

Taking a deep breath, she tightened her grip on the microphone. "Okay, Steve. Let's go."

Without waiting for a reply, she hurried toward her quarry and planted herself in his path.

Twin grooves dented Cal Richards' brow when he noticed her, but he veered sideways without slowing his pace.

She moved too, staying in front of him.

His frown deepened, and he gave her a swift but thorough perusal before homing in on the microphone in her hand and the camera operator behind her.

"Excuse me. I have work to do." His words were polite. His tone wasn't.

Stomach clenching, Amy forced herself to stand firm. "So do I. And I was hoping you'd help me do it."

"I don't give interviews."

"I just have a couple of questions. It will only take a minute of your time."

"I don't have a minute—and I don't give interviews. If you'll excuse—"

"Mr. Richards, this trial is going to get publicity whether you cooperate or not." She willed her voice to remain steady and professional. "But you could add a valuable perspective to the coverage."

His jaw hardened. "As I said before, Ms. …?"

"Winter. Amy Winter." She added the call letters of her station.

"As I said before, Ms. Winter, I don't give interviews. Not before, not during, not after a trial. So you'll save us both a lot of trouble if you accept that right now."

Before she could respond, he sidestepped her, covered the distance to the courthouse door in a few long strides, and disappeared inside.

Dang.

Expelling a frustrated breath, Amy turned to Steve, who gave her an I-told-you-so shrug. "Fine. You warned me."

"Cal Richards has a reputation for never bending the rules—his own or the law's. Everyone in the news game knows that. Did you see anyone else even *try* to talk to him?"

No, she hadn't. The other reporters in front of the courthouse, most longtime veterans of the Atlanta news scene, hadn't even approached the man. They'd obviously learned a lesson she had yet to master after only six months in town.

But if she was ever going to win the local anchor spot she'd set her sights on, and ultimately a network feature job, she had to find a way to make her coverage stand out. This story had the potential to help her do that. Getting Cal Richards' cooperation would be a coup that could boost her up at least a couple of rungs on the career ladder.

She angled toward the door the man had entered.

Maybe Steve was right. Maybe the assistant prosecuting attorney wouldn't bend. Then again, maybe he would. And until she tried everything she could think of to convince him to talk to her, she wasn't about to let Cal Richards off the hook.

* * *

Cal closed the door behind him, tossed his briefcase on the couch, and loosened his tie.

What a frustrating and unproductive day of jury selection.

No surprise, given the high-profile nature of this trial. Whenever a public figure had a run-in with the law, it was big news. Especially when that public figure was a popular sports hero like Jamie Johnson, and the manslaughter charge was so explosive.

Cal raked his fingers through his hair and paced over to the window of his apartment.

If any average citizen had been involved in a drunk-driving accident that left a pedestrian dead, they'd get the book thrown at them. But Jamie Johnson had public sentiment on his side. And since the victim was a homeless drifter, the man's death was being treated as no great loss.

Which was wrong. Manslaughter was manslaughter. It didn't matter who the victim was.

But Johnson was going to walk unless they came up with a rock-solid witness. While the sports hero didn't dispute the drunk-driving charge, his claim that the victim had stepped off the curb and into his path was hard to refute without an eyewitness. And with his clean-cut good looks and apparent sincerity and remorse, the public was buying everything Johnson was selling—despite the fact that he'd had other minor run-ins with the law, was known to be a drinker, and had demonstrated his irresponsibility in any number of ways the police were well aware of.

Cal expelled a breath and shoved his hands into his pockets.

He'd wager six months' salary the man was lying about this incident.

Unfortunately, instincts got him nowhere. He needed admissible evidence.

Leaning a shoulder against the window frame, he surveyed the city below.

There were many things he liked about his job, but the harsh reality of this kind of trial, where the odds of seeing justice done were minuscule, wasn't one of them.

Of course he'd do his best. He always did. But he'd been in this profession long enough to learn that idealism eventually gave way to disillusionment. There were just too many instances when the little guy, for lack of money or power, was shortchanged by the law—no matter how hard someone worked on their behalf.

Fighting back a wave of dejection, he gave the glittering lights another scan, willing the tension in his shoulders to ease. It was a pretty view. One his infrequent visitors always admired. But it wasn't home, and it never would be. Nor did the steel-and-concreate cityscape help him relax.

So instead, he closed his eyes and pictured the evening mist on the blue-hued mountains outside Gram's cabin in Tennessee. Called up the memory of the fresh breeze on his face, the faint, woodsy aroma of smoke curling from distant chimneys, the whisper of the wind in the pine trees, and the call of the birds.

Slowly his mind stilled and peace filled his soul.

Better.

And as soon as this trial ended, he was going home for a visit. To regroup. Refresh. Do some serious thinking about—

His cell began to vibrate, and he pulled it out of his pocket.

Unknown caller.

He ignored it. Everyone who mattered was in his contact list. This would likely be a hang-up.

Phone still in hand, he headed toward the kitchen as his stomach growled.

Yeah, yeah. It was way past dinnertime. But the prospect of a nuked meal held little appeal. The food he subsisted on was nothing like the from-scratch cooking Gram plied him with whenever he went home for a visit.

He started to set his phone on the counter. Paused at the voicemail notification on the screen.

Ignoring his protesting stomach, he played the message back.

"Mr. Richards, this is Amy Winter. We met this morning at the courthouse. I don't like to bother people outside of business hours, but I haven't had any luck connecting with you at your office and I'd like to continue our discussion. As I told you, I'm covering the Johnson trial, and your input would add a valuable perspective to the coverage. I realize, of course, that you can't discuss the trial in any detail, but perhaps you can suggest an angle I might investigate or offer some other insights that would be helpful. My cell number will be in your call log, but let me give it to you verbally too."

As she proceeded to do so, Cal scowled.

Reporters in general were bad enough, but pushy reporters like Amy Winter were the worst.

How had the woman managed to get his carefully guarded number, which was both unpublished and unlisted? And did she really think he'd return this call when he'd ignored both of the messages she'd left at his office earlier in the day?

Gritting his teeth, he erased the message. Deleted her number from his log.

Obviously she was new on the courthouse beat or she'd know that his "no comment" meant exactly that.

But she'd learn.

In the meantime, if she continued to call him, he could always file a harassment complaint. Because he didn't have time to play games.

And sooner or later, she'd get that message.

* * *

Apparently it was going to be later.

As Cal spotted the persistent reporter on the courthouse steps the next morning, he tightened his grip on his briefcase.

At least she'd left the camera operator back at the station this time.

He kept walking when she strode over and fell into step beside him.

"Good morning, Mr. Richards."

He studied her out of the corner of his eye.

Her cheeks were flushed in the chilly, early spring air, her stylish shoulder-length light brown hair ruffling in the breeze. The jade-colored jacket that screamed designer was a perfect match for her eyes, and her lashes were almost indecently long.

Conclusion?

His nemesis was a very attractive woman.

But that seemed to be a prerequisite for broadcast news these days. As far as he was concerned, TV stations would be better off if they paid more attention to solid reporting skills and real news and less to cosmetics and sensationalism.

He ignored her and picked up his pace.

"If this keeps up, I'll have to wear my running shoes next time." She lengthened her stride, matching him step for step.

He stopped so abruptly that she was a step ahead of him before she realized he'd paused.

When she turned back he gave her his most formidable glare. "I'm hoping there won't be a next time. As I told you yesterday, I don't talk to the press. And I did not appreciate you calling my cell phone. I consider that invasion of privacy, and if it happens again, I'll file a complaint. Is that understood?"

Her flush deepened, and some odd flash of emotion darted through her eyes. It was there and gone too fast to make a solid ID, but the word *cringe* came to mind.

That had to be a misread, though. Reporters were a thick-skinned bunch. You couldn't hurt their feelings or upset them if you tried.

She smoothed a hand down her jacket. "I'm sorry about the call to your cell phone. It seemed like a good idea at the time, but it won't happen again. However, I won't promise to stop calling your office or talking to you here at the courthouse. That's my job." She tilted her chin up, giving him a clear view of her classic bone structure, intelligent eyes, and full lips.

His gaze lingered on her lips a moment too long before he jerked it away. "And my job is to see justice done." He moved forward once again.

"Why should our two jobs be incompatible? And why do you hate the press so much?" She fell in beside him again, half jogging to keep up with his long strides.

He stopped at the door of the courthouse and turned to her. "They shouldn't be. Justice should be a mutual goal of the press and the law. But the only things TV stations care about are ratings and advertising revenues. If that means sensationalizing a trial at the expense of justice to gain viewers, so be it."

Her eyebrows peaked. "That's a pretty cynical attitude."

"More like realistic. How long have you been in this business, Ms. Winter? Two years? Three?"

"Seven."

Seriously?

She didn't look more than a year or two out of college. But with that kind of tenure, she had to be closer to thirty.

"Then you should know that it's hard enough to see justice done when everything works as it should. It's impossible when the press takes sides."

"You sound like you're speaking from personal experience."

He hesitated.

While he was under no obligation to explain his comment, maybe if he did she'd understand his perspective and back off.

A long shot, but worth a try.

"I am. Five years ago I handled a trial very similar to this one. High-profile figure, well liked. He was charged with rape. He was also the proverbial golden boy. Popular, wealthy, powerful, a churchgoing man with a list of philanthropic endeavors to rival Albert Schweitzer. He had the press eating out of his hand.

In fact, the news media did everything it could to discredit and harass the victim. She finally caved under the pressure. We didn't stand a chance." Despite his attempt to corral it, bitterness crept into his voice.

"So he walked."

"Yes. But two years ago he was charged with rape again—and that time he picked the wrong victim and the wrong place. She was a fighter, and she was determined to make him pay. There were also witnesses."

"So in the end, justice prevailed."

"No thanks to the press. And it depends on what you mean by justice. Yes, he was convicted. But he's still appealing. Worst case, he'll serve a couple of years and be back on the streets. I hardly consider that justice, given the crime."

Amy cocked her head. "So why did you go into law if the system is so flawed?"

He ought to brush her off. End this conversation.

Instead, for reasons that eluded him, he responded. "I hoped I could make a difference. And once in a great while, I can. Every now and then, because of my efforts, justice is served and the little guy wins. That's what keeps me going. That's what makes it worthwhile."

A hint of what looked like admiration sparked in her eyes. "Your commitment to justice is impressive."

At her compliment, warmth radiated through him.

Which was ridiculous.

Amy Winter's opinion of him was meaningless.

He straightened his shoulders and kept his expression stern. "Justice is important. I can't stop you from covering this trial, but I can—and do—decline to participate. I'll give you one piece of advice, though. Don't fall into the trap those reporters did in the case I just told you about. Don't be taken in by appearances. Do your homework. Dig. Don't assume that the image Jamie Johnson projects publicly is the real man. You'll do everyone a great service if you treat him as you would any other defendant. Try to go for substance over sensationalism."

A beat ticked by as she considered him. "No matter what I do, I have a feeling nothing will change your mind about the news game."

"When somebody dies, it's not a game."

Faint spots of color bloomed on her cheeks at his harsh tone. "Bad choice of words. But I appreciate your candor and suggestions. I'd welcome any other input you have as the trial progresses too."

"Don't hold your breath. I stay as far away from the press as possible."

"I'll keep trying, you know."

Yeah, he did.

Shrugging, he turned away. "Suit yourself."

But she wasn't going to get any more out of him.

Not a word.

No matter how hard she tried.

About the Author

© DeWeesePhotography.com

Irene Hannon is the bestselling, award-winning author of more than sixty-five contemporary romance and romantic suspense novels. She is also a three-time winner of the RITA award—the "Oscar" of romance fiction—from Romance Writers of America, and a member of that organization's elite Hall of Fame.

Her many other awards include National Readers' Choice, Daphne du Maurier, Retailers' Choice, Booksellers' Best, Carol, and Reviewer's Choice from *RT Book Reviews* magazine, which also honored her with a Career Achievement award for her entire body of work. In addition, she is a HOLT medallion winner and a two-time Christy award finalist.

Millions of copies of her books have been sold worldwide, and her novels have been translated into multiple languages.

Irene, who holds a BA in psychology and an MA in journalism, juggled two careers for many years until she gave up her executive corporate communications position with a Fortune 500 company to write full-time. She is happy to say she has no regrets.

A trained vocalist, Irene has sung the leading role in numerous community musical theater productions and is a soloist at her church. She and her husband enjoy traveling, hiking, gardening, and spending time with family. They make their home in Missouri.

To learn more about Irene and her books, visit www.irenehannon.com. She loves to interact with readers on Facebook and is also active on Instagram.

Printed in Dunstable, United Kingdom

82409174R00122